Novels by ANDREW GREY

Accompanied by a Waltz
Crossing Divides
Dutch Treat
A Heart Without Borders
In Search of a Story
Inside Out
One Good Deed
Stranded • Taken
Three Fates (anthology)
Work Me Out (anthology)

ART SERIES
Legal Artistry • Artistic Appeal • Artistic Pursuits • Legal Tender

BOTTLED UP STORIES
Bottled Up • Uncorked • The Best Revenge • An Unexpected Vintage

THE BULLRIDERS
A Daring Ride • A Wild Ride

CHILDREN OF BACCHUS STORIES
Children of Bacchus • Thursday's Child • Child of Joy

GOOD FIGHT SERIES
The Good Fight • The Fight Within • The Fight for Identity

LOVE MEANS… SERIES
Love Means… No Shame • Love Means… Courage • Love Means… No Boundaries
Love Means… Freedom • Love Means … No Fear
Love Means… Family • Love Means… Renewal • Love Means… No Limits

Published by DREAMSPINNER PRESS
http://www.dreamspinnerpress.com

Published by DREAMSPINNER PRESS
http://www.dreamspinnerpress.com

Readers Love Andrew Grey

A Heart Without Borders

"I felt like I was right there with the characters, feeling the heat, the desperation and the total devastation right along with them. There is no doubt in my mind that this book will stay with me for a long time."

—The Novel Approach

"In true Andrew Grey fashion, this book delivers not only a romance but a powerful lesson on the courage, hope and optimism of people in a country devastated by disaster and poverty."

—Hearts on Fire Reviews

Stranded

"A great story of how time passes and people allow their relationship to settle into routine and they lose their appreciation for their partner. This doesn't mean that they are no longer deeply in love, sometimes they just need a reminder."

—Gay List Book Reviews

"*Stranded* is an amazing combination between an intense thriller-like stalker story, a sizzling romance, and a character study which, through tension and drama, brings out the worst and the best in both main characters."

—Rainbow Book Reviews

A Daring Ride

"All the things we've come to love from Grey are there in the print. An emotional, engrossing, and sexy ride is what's in store with this latest work from one of the best authors in the genre."

—MM Good Book Reviews

"I quickly got sucked in by the story and the characters. There really is so much substance in the plot and the people… he doesn't need a lot of extra language to pull you in."

—Mrs. Condit & Friends Read Books

Readers Love Andrew Grey

An Isolated Range

"Mr. Grey delivers a highly emotional story that captures the reader's heart in one fell swoop. This is an author who is dedicated to his series, stories and characters. With each range story, you always find yourself drawn in, breathless until the very last page is read."
—Dawn's Reading Nook

"Andrew Grey's Range series just gets stronger with each new book and *An Isolated Range* is perhaps the most amazing addition yet."
—Scattered Thoughts and Rogue Words

"*An Isolated Range* is a story not of human triumphs but also of sadness and death. This is an author who balances both so well that the reader is left speechless after that last page is read."
—Love Romances and More

The Fight Within

"I loved this book, these characters, and this story. Get it today. Read. Understand and through understanding, enjoy."
—Mrs. Condit & Friends Read Books

"This is a story that is rich in detail, delving into the Native American culture and also sharing the suffering that the Native American's still face today."
—MM Good Book Reviews

"This was a very powerful read."
—Live your Life, Buy the Book

LOVE COMES
Home

ANDREW GREY

Dreamspinner Press

Published by
Dreamspinner Press
5032 Capital Circle SW
Suite 2, PMB# 279
Tallahassee, FL 32305-7886
USA
http://www.dreamspinnerpress.com/

Love Comes Home
© 2014 Andrew Grey.

Cover Art
© 2014 Cover Art by L.C. Chase.
http://www.lcchase.com
Cover content is for illustrative purposes only and any person depicted on the cover is a model.

ISBN: 978-1-62798-661-8
Digital ISBN: 978-1-62798-662-5

Printed in the United States of America
First Edition
March 2014

To my husband, Dominic. We're legal now!

CHAPTER
One

"KEEP YOUR eye on the ball, Davey," Greg Hampton called from the bleachers of his son's Little League game. "I know you can do it!"

Davey turned toward him and nodded.

Greg ignored the way the players on the other team moved in as he concentrated and hoped that this time Davey would connect with the ball and hit it out of the ballpark. That was every father's dream—to see his son excel at something the way he had. Greg had played baseball in college and had been scouted by more than one professional team. He'd even gotten an offer, but at the same time he'd also gotten a job proposal from a nationally known architectural firm as a draftsman. They'd offered him a good salary and a chance to continue his education so he could become an architect like his father. So he'd taken the job and put his baseball dreams on the shelf. In retrospect, it had been a good decision.

Baseball—professional baseball—was competitive beyond belief. He'd been a good player, but looking back, he could see he would never have been a great player. Instead, he was a great architect. People sought him out for his home designs, which were innovative takes on the classics. He'd designed Cotswold cottages for placement in Chicago, Swiss chalets with all the charm on the outside and incredible living spaces inside. He'd even designed a chateau for a famous billionaire that looked like it belonged in the French countryside and was hundreds of years old, but sat on a hundred acres of gardens and lawns just outside Grand Rapids, Michigan. Greg was a winner, and he wanted his son to be a winner at the game he'd loved so much.

"Is that your son?" one of the fathers sitting next to him asked.

"Yeah." Greg grinned, glancing at the man and then turning back to Davey. "You can do it," he called again as a helmeted Davey took the plate. His swing looked good, just like Greg had taught him, and his practice swings looked powerful. The elements were all there, but the first pitch came and Davey swung hard, getting nothing but air. "That's okay. Take your time and wait for your pitch!" Davey stepped back to the plate and got into position. He fanned again, and on the next pitch, as well, before heading back to the dugout. "That's okay. You'll get them next time."

Greg watched the next player come to bat, and the game continued. He rooted for each player in turn, making sure all the kids were cheered on. Greg knew some of the fathers weren't able to make every game and he remembered how he felt when he was young, making a great play or hitting a home run with no one there to see it.

The innings passed, and Davey came up to bat again.

"He's swinging too late," the man next to him said.

"I know. We worked on that all week, and I thought we had his timing down better," Greg said.

"I'm not complaining, just observing," the man said. "Jerry Fisher," he added, holding out his hand. Greg shook it and introduced himself. "Has he been doing that long?"

"No. It's something that started happening this season. Last year he was a good hitter, but he moved up, and I think the more advanced pitches are getting to him," Greg said. "I'll work with him some more this week. He'll get it."

"Do you work with him a lot?" Jerry asked.

"A couple times a week. I played in college and I want him to love the game, so I don't think at ten it's good to push. It needs to be fun," Greg said. "But we all know winning is a lot more fun than losing."

Jerry nodded. "That's my nephew," Jerry said as Bobby, one of Davey's teammates, came up to bat. "My sister and brother-in-law are out of town, so I'm nephew-sitting." Jerry smiled. "Has the team lost a lot?"

Greg turned back to the game when he heard a sharp crack and saw Bobby run off toward first. The bleachers broke into cheers as the ball sailed over the fence for a home run.

"No," Greg said. But he knew when you weren't playing well and didn't feel as though you were contributing, the wins didn't feel like yours. He said nothing and did his best to be encouraging.

The game continued, inning after inning, until Davey and his teammates celebrated their win. Greg waited for Davey, ruffling his son's hair when he approached. "Is the team going anywhere to celebrate?"

"Pizza," Davey answered.

"Well, then, let's go," Greg told him. He said good-bye to Jerry and followed Davey to the car.

Davey was quiet the entire ride to the pizza place. As soon as they arrived, some of Davey's teammates met him at the car, jumping and shouting. Davey joined in, and Greg hoped, at least for now, the memories of Davey's strikeouts would recede.

The boys went inside and sat together at a large table in the back. Greg joined the dads, opened his wallet, and handed a twenty to the guy in charge. The order was pretty standard, and once placed, the coaches and parents took tables near the players to act as a buffer between them and the other patrons. Jerry sat across from him, and Greg used the opportunity to scope the man out a little. He was sort of cute, but Greg didn't let his thoughts travel too far.

When the food arrived, the din from behind him settled down as the boys started to eat. The pizza for the adults arrived a few minutes later, and Greg's stomach rumbled at the sight of the loaded pizza. He placed a slice on his plate and waited for the others to get theirs before taking a second slice.

"I wanted to speak to you if I could," Jerry said when the others were involved in a discussion of some proposed rule changes.

"Sure," Greg said. He'd had more than one conversation start like that, and it usually centered around the "gay thing," as one man had put it. He took a bite and waited for Jerry to continue.

"I don't do this lightly, but have you had Davey's eyes checked?" Jerry asked and then reached into his pocket and pulled out a card. "I'm not trying to drum up business—I'll examine him for free."

"He wears glasses," Greg said.

"I'm an ophthalmologist, not an optometrist. I won't charge you for the visit," Jerry repeated.

"You think there's something wrong?" Greg's stomach clenched.

"I don't know. But you have nothing to lose by having him checked. Like I said, I'll do it for free," Jerry said.

Greg nodded and looked down at the card. He read it and then placed it in his pocket. "I'll call next week," he said, not really believing his answer. But Jerry had started him wondering, and it grew until they got home, when Greg picked up his phone and dialed the number on the card. He left a message on the machine for Jerry and requested a callback. He got one first thing the following morning.

A WEEK later, Greg drove Davey to his appointment.

"Why are we doing this, Dad?" Davey asked, fidgeting in the front seat. "I can see just fine."

Ever since Greg made the appointment, Davey had gone out of his way to demonstrate how well he could see, but Greg noticed little things, like Davey moving closer to a book and then pushing it away when he saw his father watching. Greg didn't want to argue and thought Davey probably just needed a different prescription. When they arrived at Jerry's office, the receptionist took their information, and Greg filled out a bunch of forms. But she didn't ask for any sort of payment or even an insurance card.

"David Hampton," the nurse called after a while, and she led them down a hallway of examining rooms. People passed them going in and out for eye exams, and she led Greg and Davey back farther, into a room next to an office with Jerry's name on the door. "Please have a seat there," she instructed. Davey and Greg settled in the plastic chairs off to the side.

They didn't have to wait long before Jerry came in. He sat on his stool and immediately began talking to Davey. "There's nothing to worry about. None of what we're going to do today is going to hurt. But I am going to shine a light into your eyes and have a good look around. I'm also going to run a few standard tests, and then, based on those, we might do some others. Okay?" he said to Davey, who looked at Greg and then back at the doctor and nodded.

"Good. I saw you play the other week," Jerry said as he got his instruments ready. A nurse came in and settled at the counter behind Jerry. "This is Annette. She'll be helping me today." Davey smiled nervously. "When I saw you playing, I noticed that you were swinging late, and your dad said you didn't have that problem last year."

"No. I was hitting good last year. At least, Coach said I was," Davey answered.

"Have you had any troubles seeing in school? Do you sit closer to the front now so you can see?" Jerry asked and slid his chair closer to Davey. Greg saw his son tense.

"Nothing to worry about. It's just a light. Will you take your glasses off for me?" Davey did and handed them to Jerry, who passed them to Annette.

"We have assigned seats in school," Davey said.

"Have you found school harder this year?"

"Yeah," Davey answered. "It's fifth grade."

Jerry nodded. "Look at the chart over my shoulder and don't follow the light. Just watch the chart. That's good." Jerry alternated talking to Davey and speaking to Annette in what must have been eye doctor code. He continued working with Davey, looking at his eyes through various kinds of equipment. He did the puff test, which Davey did better at than Greg ever did. It was the worst part of his eye exam.

Greg tried not to be nervous as the exam continued. Jerry did the various eye chart tests as well as some Greg had never seen before.

"I'm going to dilate your eyes with some drops. It will feel funny for a while, but I need to do this to get a better look. It doesn't hurt, but when you leave, we can give you some temporary sunglasses because you'll be extra sensitive to light."

Davey agreed, and they went through the rest of the exam. When Jerry was done, he said good-bye to Davey. "The nurse will help you out to the waiting room. I'd like to talk to your dad for a few minutes."

Davey got up and left with Annette, who closed the door behind them.

"I'd like to run some additional tests," Jerry said. "David's vision with his glasses is about twenty/forty; without them he's twenty/one hundred. How old are these glasses?"

Greg thought for a few seconds. "Less than a year. Why, did they get the prescription wrong?"

"I'd like you to tell me where you had them made and give me permission to have his records transferred here. But I doubt they got the prescription that wrong. Instead, it appears that David's vision has deteriorated considerably in the last eight months. Those glasses should have given him twenty/twenty vision. They didn't say anything to you otherwise when you had the glasses made?"

Greg shook his head.

"Don't worry at this point," Jerry said. "I'll have you sign the forms so I can get the records, and once I do, I'll call you. We can also set up an appointment for the tests I need."

"Can't you do them here?"

"No. These need a radiologist. I want a CT scan of the back of David's eyes."

"You really think there's something wrong with his eyes?" Greg asked. He swallowed hard, his stomach clenching with worry.

"Quite honestly I'm concerned about the apparent deterioration in his vision. I won't be sure until I get the records from his previous exam as well as the results of the tests I'd like to do, but I do have concerns." Jerry paused. "I don't want to make a diagnosis based on incomplete information. We'll get the tests scheduled as quickly as we can so we can get some answers. I promise." Jerry nodded for emphasis, stood up, and opened the door.

Greg walked out front, and Jerry followed. Jerry gave the receptionist some instructions, and they helped get the appointments set up. Greg signed the forms for the release of the records and then joined Davey in the waiting room.

"Let's go home," he said with a touch of excitement he didn't feel. Davey nodded and slowly got up, and they left the office. They walked to the car in silence and got in.

"Dad, what did the doctor want? Is something wrong?" Panic edged Davey's voice.

Greg didn't have answers and figured the truth, or at least part of it, was the best way to go. "He wants to run some more tests. He saw something but isn't sure what it is. We're going to have your records transferred, and the tests should tell them what's going on." He shifted toward his son, watching Davey blink his blue eyes as he stared back. Greg leaned over the seat and hugged Davey as best he could. He didn't know what else to do.

"It could be nothing, Dad," Davey said.

Greg knew in his heart it wasn't likely to be nothing. But they could do amazing things these days, and whatever was wrong, Greg hoped it was something correctable. He could feel Davey's nervousness as well as his own, but there was nothing they could do right now. So Greg determined to continue their lives as normally as possible until they got some answers.

OVER THE next few weeks, Davey had the tests and the records were transferred. Once the results were in, Greg and Davey sat waiting, not in an examining room, but in Jerry's office, with bookshelves behind the desk and diplomas and awards hung on the walls. Davey fidgeted in his chair, and Greg felt himself doing the same thing. Whatever came of this meeting, he knew it would be important.

"Good morning," Jerry said as he came in and closed the door before sitting behind his desk. He opened the folder in front of him and looked at Davey and then at Greg. Over the next ten minutes, Jerry explained the results of the tests and what they meant. Davey was stunned, and Greg listened as best he could, trying to take in all of the information Jerry had for them. By the end, Greg sucked hard for air as tears filled his eyes, knowing his son would eventually go blind.

CHAPTER
Two

TOM SPANGLER turned the corner and did his best to find a place to park. Ken and Patrick's party was sure hopping this year if all of these cars were here for them. He loved this time of year in Pleasanton, in Michigan's beautiful Upper Peninsula. He grabbed the bottle of wine out of the back as well as the large bowl of his grandmother's macaroni salad. After bumping the door closed with his hip, he strode across the street and around to the back.

"Ken," Tom called when he saw his friend hurrying down the walk. "Looks like you have quite the gathering." Ken opened the gate, and Tom hurried inside before following Ken toward the din of overlapping conversations.

"Did you have any trouble with the directions?" Ken asked, taking the bowl, and Tom shook his head. "I'll put this inside. There are soft drinks in the blue cooler, and the red one has wine and beer. Help yourself. I'll be right back out to make introductions."

"It's okay, I'm good at introducing myself," Tom said, looking around the gathering. "You've got your hands full," he added with a smile. Ken hurried inside, and Tom opened the beer cooler and pulled out a cold bottle of Sam Adams Summer Ale. He opened it and took a drink before beginning to circulate. If there was one thing he knew, it was how to work a room. He'd been doing it since he was ten and had been allowed to attend the first of his mother's legendary social gatherings. Every weekend there was some sort of party, either thrown by his parents or by their circle of well-heeled friends.

He turned at a light tap on the shoulder and came face-to-face with Ken's partner, Patrick. He was immediately engulfed in a hug. Patrick had been an opera singer before an accident had robbed him of his voice. Tom had never brought it up because it would be insensitive on his part, but he'd seen Patrick perform when he'd gone to Opera Cleveland with his mother.

"How are you?" Tom asked. Patrick smiled and nodded, then pointed to Tom, as if to ask him the same question. "I'm doing well. It's so great to see you again."

He couldn't help himself and hugged Patrick once again. The man was the most tactile person Tom had ever met. He was also one of the most wonderful.

"Are you working on any projects? I have a bedroom I'd like to furnish, and I'd love it if you'd make the furniture. I want a complete set—bed, dressers, nightstands, the works."

Patrick moved to the side of the deck and ran his hand over the railing. Tom nodded his understanding.

"You can use whatever wood you want. I know it will be wonderful, and you're the craftsman."

Patrick let Tom know that he'd e-mail him by making a typing motion. Tom agreed, and then Patrick was called away by one of the other guests, which was fine. He was in demand. Patrick couldn't speak, but his personality and heart were as big as all outdoors. Since Tom had met Ken and Patrick at an artists' evening fundraiser for the Red Cross almost a year earlier, he'd been jealous in a small way that Patrick was taken.

He stepped back and something bumped the back of his leg. He turned around to see a man sitting in one of the chairs, holding a white cane. "I'm sorry, I don't believe we've met. I'm Tom Spangler, a friend of Ken and Patrick's."

"Howard Justinian," the man said and held up his hand.

Tom took it in his, shaking briefly and then letting go. The chair next to Howard was empty, so he sat down.

"My partner, Gordy, is around here somewhere. You can't miss him."

"Yellow shirt, really big?" Tom said and then stopped. The white cane should have been a clue. He wanted to smack his forehead.

Howard laughed. "Don't worry about it. Yes, Gordy is big, and I think he said he was wearing yellow. Personally, I like it when people treat me like everyone else." Howard sat back in the chair. "How do you know Ken and Patrick?"

"I was involved in a fundraiser at the Red Cross last year. We were doing an artistic evening, and Ken donated one of his works and agreed to act as a sort of master of ceremonies for the evening. Since I was organizing the event, we worked together for a few weeks and got to be friends. And if you know anything about Ken and Patrick, they seem to welcome people into their lives."

"Yes, they do," Howard agreed and then turned slightly. "Gordy, this is Tom." Howard smiled. "Before you think I'm psychic, I'd know his footsteps anywhere."

Tom stood and shook hands with Gordy.

"He loves to do that," Gordy said and turned to Howard. "Token is out in the yard, watching the kids."

"Token, come," Howard said, and Tom watched as a German shepherd walked across the yard and up the stairs onto the deck before sitting at Howard's feet.

"That's really something," one of the men a few chairs away said.

Howard picked up the harness between their chairs. Tom hadn't even noticed it. He laid it out, and Token stepped into the openings so Howard could pull it up and fasten it around him. Then he curled up at Howard's feet. Every minute or so, he'd look up at Howard and then relax.

"Do you mind if I interrupt?" the man asked, moving his chair closer. "I'm Greg Hampton, and I couldn't help noticing your dog."

"Token is a trained Seeing Eye dog," Howard said. Gordy sat down on the other side of Howard and entwined their fingers. "I've had him two years now." Howard lightly stroked the dog's head.

"Sometimes I wonder if he's more attached to him or me," Gordy joked, and Howard lightly bumped against the large man. It was obvious to Tom that wasn't the case at all.

Greg looked uncomfortable, and Tom wondered if it was from being around Howard. "How would I go about getting a dog like that for my son?" The pain in Greg's voice hit Tom hard.

"Is he blind?" Howard asked.

"Not yet," Greg answered. Tom glanced at the others around them and then shifted his gaze back to Greg.

"If you want to talk about it, you're in the right group," Howard said, leaning forward slightly.

"Dad, I hit the ball," a boy said as he approached. He stood in front of Greg. "The boys were playing baseball, and I hit it. It was a good hit too."

"That's great, Davey," Greg said. Tom could hear the enthusiasm in his voice and saw the excitement in Greg's eyes, but it seemed hollow to him. Thankfully, Davey didn't seem to notice. "Go back to the game and have fun."

Davey whispered something.

"You can have one, but you have to drink it all."

Davey opened the soda cooler and leaned in close. He pulled out a can and then put it back before picking up another one. Eventually he closed the lid. When he turned around, the first thing Tom saw were Davey's Coke-bottle glasses. The boy hurried off, nearly stumbling on the stairs. Greg winced and held still until Davey ran across the grass. Then he got up and walked across the deck to stand by the railing, watching the kids play.

"It can be very hard on parents when they find out their child is going blind," Howard said from next to him.

Tom continued watching Greg, his heart unable to allow him to look away. "Could you... were you...?" Tom began.

"It's fine. I don't remember ever being able to see. I was told once that there was the possibility I might have been able to see when I was born, but I think that was wishful thinking on my parents' part. Nonetheless, it was hard on them, and if Davey is going blind, it will be hard on his dad."

Tom stood up. "Excuse me," he said softly. He got another beer and then decided to grab two. He walked over to Greg and nudged his arm, offering the second beer. Greg took it with a slight nod, but said nothing as he twisted off the top. Sometimes a guy didn't need to talk. Sometimes, and Tom figured this was one of those times, a guy just needed someone to stand quietly by his side.

"He used to be so active," Greg said, placing the empty bottle on the railing. "Now, seeing him run and play like that is a rarity. He sits two feet from the television and watches it all the time."

"What happened?"

Greg sighed. "No one knows. They think it's probably genetic. He reached a certain age and the aberrant genes kicked in or something. Last year he was largely normal, playing baseball like any other kid. This spring his playing got more difficult and I took him to an ophthalmologist. This year I've gotten him three pairs of glasses in nine months, each one stronger than the last. But they only help him for a little while." Greg turned toward him. "Three months ago, when I got him these glasses, he could read and was actually doing things, but slowly the books got closer to his face, and he got closer to the television. His world is going darker by the day, and there's nothing I can do about it."

"Maybe you can't stop him from going blind. But you can help him adjust to his circumstances," Tom said, and then he realized how he sounded. "Sorry, didn't mean to sound preachy."

"It's nothing I haven't told myself multiple times. I want to give him everything I wasn't able to have."

"You still can. He's going to need you more than he ever has," Tom said. "Not that I know what it's like to be blind or to have a kid go blind, but I know about wanting a parent's love and attention and not getting it. So I can say from experience that's the most important thing."

Tom jumped when he heard a voice behind him.

"You have it within your power to help make the transition from sighted to unsighted person truly hell or something your son can learn to live with and eventually thrive in spite of. And he will thrive. How quickly that happens is up to you as well as to him."

Tom turned around and saw Howard standing just behind him.

"I can do most anything a sighted person can do. Yes, there are limitations, but the world isn't closed off to me. It's just different from the one you have." Howard looked upward. "Did you notice the squirrel in the tree above us?" They all lifted their gazes and saw a squirrel jumping from limb to limb.

"No, I didn't," Greg admitted.

"Neither did I," Tom said as he watched the acrobat.

"I heard him. He's been playing and chattering up there for the past half hour. Like I said, the world isn't closed or smaller—it's just different. I have difficulty getting around in strange places. That's why I have Token. He guides me and helps keep me away from trouble. Gordy is there for me too." Howard moved closer, holding Token's harness. "I will warn you, though. Your instinct as a parent is to protect Davey from everything you can. The thing is, you're going to have to let him explore the world in a whole new way, and you won't be able to keep him from danger. You have to let him find things out on his own. Guide, but don't sequester. My family protected me nearly to the point where they were cutting me off from the world. I rebelled, and things weren't so good for a while."

"But he's ten," Greg said.

"And as a sighted person, he's finding his way. You have to let him do that same thing as a blind person," Howard told him. "Before we leave, I'll have Gordy give you my phone number. I'd be happy to talk to you some more, and talk with Davey if you like."

"That would be nice, thank you," Greg said.

"Anytime," Howard said and then slowly descended the stairs with Token on one side and Gordy on the other.

A little girl raced across the yard to them, pigtails flying. Gordy caught her and lifted her up as she laughed.

Tom wasn't sure if Greg wanted to talk and figured he'd leave him alone, but then Greg said, "Davey was always into sports. Now what is he going to do?"

Tom shrugged. "Google 'sports for the blind' or find out if there are programs for kids who are sight impaired. There have to be some in this area. It might be good for him to be with other kids who have the same problem he does."

"You think?"

"Yeah. Sometimes with kids they just need to know they aren't the only one in the world with that particular problem." Tom knew that feeling well too. He'd hidden who he was from his family for a long time. None of their friends were gay, and their circle was so closed and limited that he rarely got to see outside of it until he was out of the house. Then the world that opened up to him had been eye-opening.

"You sound like you're speaking from experience," Greg observed.

"I was. The whole gay thing really threw me as a kid. I really thought I was the only person in the world like this. My parents never talked about things like that with me. Hell, they didn't talk about much with me. They were too caught up in their parties, benefits, and causes. I was raised by nannies until I was ten or eleven, and then I was more or less just around. Mom and Dad were there, but still wrapped up in their lives. So I was left to figure things out on my own or hear stuff from the other kids." Tom shrugged. The past was the past and he really didn't want to dwell on it or complain about it while at a party. "How about we join the party and have a good time? They're setting up a volleyball net. If you grab Davey, we could make a good team."

"Yeah, let's," Greg said. "But I need another beer for that."

It seemed as though they both did. Maybe volleyball was better with a buzz. He wasn't sure, but the few beers seemed to make the game more fun. They played for about an hour, until Ken called that the food was ready. The guests formed a line and filled their plates, then sat on the chairs, at tables, or on blankets on the lawn. Tom settled for a spot in the shade. Greg and Davey joined him, still a little flushed from the game, but happy and smiling.

"What do you do?" Greg asked him.

"I'm a sort of money manager," Tom answered vaguely. "And you?"

"Architect," Greg answered.

"Wait a minute, you… are you *the* Greg Hampton?" Tom asked with a grin.

"You know who I am?" Greg asked. Most people outside architecture circles had probably never heard of him. It wasn't like he'd designed a famous building like I. M. Pei or Santiago Calatrava.

"You designed a home—" Tom couldn't help snickering. "Maybe it would be best to call it a mansion-slash-castle—for some friends of my parents. They raved about you."

Greg smiled. "That's nice to hear, and I remember that job. It was an interesting building with definite challenges. I swore they wanted Hearst Castle on a McMansion budget." Greg's smile faded. "Sorry, I shouldn't talk about clients that way, especially if they're friends of your family."

"No. The Fosters are cheap. They made their money the old-fashioned way: inheritance. And they've kept it the even older way: they pinch every penny. King Midas has nothing on those people." Tom chuckled silently to himself, remembering the time he'd gone over to their huge house to play and the only toys the kids had were ones their mother had picked up at yard sales. Half of them were broken, but it was all the kids had. "But they were certainly impressed with you, and they love the house." Tom had loved the house from the outside as well. The inside, not so much, but he'd always blamed that on the Fosters and their cheapness, not the architect. The spaces inside had definite bones of grandeur, but the cheap furnishings and ugly carpet pulled the eye.

"Dad's working on a cottage now. I want him to do one just like it for me someday," Davey said. He'd been quiet while he slowly ate.

"You bet, Davey," Greg said, tugging his son into a light man hug. It wasn't long before the kids were running and playing again. Davey finished eating and joined them. "He's having a great time."

"I know you're worried, but he seems to be adjusting pretty well," Tom observed.

"Davey compensates, but there are things he can't compensate for." Greg sighed. "Sorry, I don't want to just talk about my problems. This is a party, after all."

"It certainly is," Ken said as he approached. "That means there's plenty more food, and dessert will be brought out in a little while." Ken looked like he might join them, but then Tom turned around and saw Patrick signaling for Ken's attention. "I'll talk to you in a few minutes," Ken said. He hurried away, and Tom and Greg found themselves alone once again.

Tom hadn't figured that Greg was gay, him having a son and all, but when he turned back around, he realized he was being checked out. Not that he minded in the least. Greg was handsome, trim with rich blue eyes and brown, wavy hair. Tom had always liked the old silent movies, and Greg reminded him of one of those stars, with his great cheekbones and incredibly expressive face. He looked away when Tom caught him peeking. Tom lightly touched Greg's hand to let him know it was okay.

Greg smiled at the gesture.

"Can I ask you something? If it's too personal, you don't have to answer. I'm assuming you're gay," Tom said a little nervously, in case his gaydar was way the hell off.

Greg nodded. "How did I get Davey?"

"Yeah. There has to be a story there," Tom said. He loved a good story. As a kid, he used to wear his nannies hoarse asking them to read him "one more story."

Greg shrugged. "I was married."

Tom's eyebrows rose.

"It was total stupidity on my part. I got Davey's mother pregnant, and her father very nearly came at me with a shotgun. I did the right things and married her." Greg looked up into the canopy of leaves overhead. "It was both a mistake and the best thing I ever did in my life. Joyce was the mistake part. Once the honeymoon was over, and that happened dang fast, we were at each other's throats. It got better between us once she had the baby, and we stayed together for a year after that. I was busy trying to build my career and reputation, while Joyce only wanted to cat around. Turned out I was only the guy who married her."

"So is Davey yours?" Tom asked.

"Yes. She tried to claim he wasn't during the divorce, but I had tests done, and he's definitely mine." Greg smiled. "That actually worked in my favor, because after that I sued for full custody on moral and behavioral grounds. She'd admitted to sleeping around, and my lawyer pulled in a parade of guys she'd been with. Seemed none of them liked her very much out of the sack," Greg added with a certain amount of glee. "The nail in Joyce's coffin was when one of her friends came forward and testified that she'd told her the only reason she was fighting for custody was to get the child support. Joyce's friend said on the stand that Davey would have a better life with me than he ever would with Joyce."

"Wow. Does he ever see her?" Tom asked, shifting his gaze to where Davey was playing. He saw Greg do the same and loved the smile that curled on his lips.

"Sometimes. Officially she has visitation, but she lives in Florida now and she hasn't exercised those rights in a while. I told her about Davey's vision, and I could swear I heard nothing but relief. She has her career and her own life now—thankfully, no more children." Greg shook his head. "I can't understand how she could walk away from her own child. If it had been me and the courts had ruled the other way, I'd still be fighting for Davey."

Tom heard the hitch in Greg's voice. "A few years ago I had a boyfriend. At the time Charles and I were pretty serious. We were about to move in together and had talked about children. But...." Tom shrugged. "Things went sour after that." He tried not to sound bitter and played down all the reasons why things had gone bad.

"I'm sorry. Davey is the best thing that ever happened to me."

"Does he know you're gay?" Tom asked.

Greg laughed. "Yes. He keeps asking me when I'm going to find a man and settle down. He says he doesn't care if he has two dads. One of the boys on his softball team has two moms, and of course he knows Ken and Patrick through Hanna."

It suddenly became quiet. Greg shifted and looked over to where the kids had been playing. Everyone stood still. Hanna, Ken's twelve-year-old daughter, was walking slowly, feeling around. Then she stopped, and Tom saw her hand Davey his glasses. "He doesn't like to talk about it, but he can only see the bare outline of things without his glasses." The kids resumed their game, but Davey walked to the edge of the group and leaned against one of the trees.

Greg stood up and continued watching.

"What's going on?" Tom asked, standing as well. He watched as Hanna spoke to Davey and then took him by the hand and led him back to where the kids were playing.

"I'm not sure," Greg said. But whatever the problem was, it was short-lived, and Davey began playing again.

"Do you work on just one commission at a time or do you have multiple projects at once?" Tom asked, hoping to change the subject.

"Nice segue," Greg said and sat back down. People began milling around on the deck, and Tom saw people descending the stairs with cake. The kids must have seen it too, because they came over en masse. "I take it you aren't in the mood to fight for cake."

"If I know Ken, there will be plenty," Tom said. "You were saying…."

"I can usually handle a number of projects at once. How many depends on their complexity. Some clients only pay me to draw up the plans and then they find a builder to execute them. Others have me involved in the project until completion. I have a network of people I can contact for some of the more specialized requirements for a design. Once, a client asked for a home with New Orleans-style iron railings, and I got them in touch with an artisan in Louisiana who was able to fabricate what they wanted. Specialized ironworkers, woodcarvers, glass artists—all of those come into play at one point or another when you design the kinds of houses I do. Last year I had a couple in Pennsylvania, just outside Pittsburgh, who wanted me to design and then supervise the construction of their home. Davey and I spent three months out there. I was able to line up other jobs, and he went to school there for a while. It was hard on both of us, but it was what he wanted. I would have turned the job down if Davey hadn't been willing to move. It turned out the client had a number of connections, so Davey went to a private school along with the client's children and they gave him a specialized curriculum, so when he came back, he hadn't missed anything."

"I bet that was something," Tom said.

"Davey didn't want to leave. It was the best school experience for him. But this is home, and it was nice coming back." Greg looked away as Davey approached, walking carefully as he balanced a number of plates.

"I brought you both cake," he said, handing them plates.

"Thank you," they both said, and Davey smiled and hurried back to where the kids had started to play again.

"He's going to sleep well tonight," Tom observed. He ate his cake and watched Greg without looking like he was watching. As they sat and ate, the shadows continued to lengthen. Tom knew soon it would be getting dark and the picnic would come to an end. "Look, I was wondering…," he began, placing his plate on the grass and then fidgeting with one of the empty beer bottles. This sort of thing always made him feel like a teenager again. "Maybe you'd like to have dinner with me sometime?" It didn't seem to matter how old he got; asking someone on a date always felt like the first time, stomach butterflies and all.

Greg didn't answer right away. "That would be nice," he said with a slight smile. "I haven't been on a date in a while. When most guys find out I have a kid, they tend to turn the other way and head for the door pretty fast."

"I'm not most guys," Tom said seriously. He reached behind him and pulled out his wallet, then handed Greg one of his cards. It was a personal one, so it simply had his name and phone number on it.

Then it was Greg's turn to fidget until he gave Tom one of his. "Use the cell number," Greg said.

Tom took the card and placed it in his wallet. "Do you want another drink?"

"No, thanks. We need to go soon, and I have to drive." Greg stood up and called to Davey.

Other parents were collecting their kids as well, so it was definitely approaching the time to leave. Tom gave Greg a hug and then released him. Greg collected Davey and then made the rounds to say good-bye, with both of them collecting hugs before leaving.

Tom wandered up to the deck and joined the others sitting around and talking.

"It looked like the two of you hit it off," Ken said.

"We did." Tom suddenly realized he'd spent the entire evening with Greg. "I hope I wasn't rude."

Both Ken and Patrick laughed and shook their heads. "Everything is fine," Ken said and sat in one of the empty chairs with a sigh. He pulled a beer out of the cooler and opened it, relaxing after playing host all afternoon. "You weren't being rude to anyone. Greg seemed to have a good time, and so did his son."

"That's good," Howard said from just across the way. "I wonder who's having a harder time with Davey losing his sight—him or his dad."

"Greg's being a dad. He's concerned for his son. No one can blame him," Ken observed.

"No, you can't," Howard agreed. "Not at all. Being blind isn't the end of the world, but it isn't the easiest thing in the world either. I can't imagine what it's like to see because I never could, but I suppose it would be like me learning I'd go deaf." Howard shuddered, and Gordy took his hand.

"Not everyone is like you," Gordy said lightly. "You're as strong as they come. Davey is a kid. He's seen the world, and that's slowly being taken away from him. It must be hard knowing you have something now, but it will eventually be gone."

"Exactly," Tom agreed. "But Davey seemed to have a good time."

"He's nice," Hanna chimed in, coming to stand next to her father. She whispered something to him, and Ken nodded. Hanna took Howard's niece, Sophia, by the hand and led her inside.

"Hanna and Sophia are going to play games," Ken told Howard.

"Are you sure it's okay for Sophia to stay the night?" Howard asked. "You must have a lot of work to do to clean up."

"Of course. They'll have a ball, and Sophia will help keep Hanna occupied so we can get done what we need to. It's mostly throwing away the trash and making sure the furniture is put away. Most people took their dishes with them, so it's no problem."

They sat and talked for another hour, then Howard and Gordy got up to leave. Tom figured that was his cue to leave as well. He got his dish, which had been scraped clean, and said good night before heading out to his car. Tom drove home and parked in the empty bay in the garage. He looked over at the two other cars and was glad he hadn't taken either of them. Sure, they were fun to drive, but for a gathering like the one this afternoon, they were a little attention-getting, and Tom wasn't out for attention, at least not today. He grabbed the empty bowl and got out, then closed the car door. Then he headed inside.

Every day he was thankful he hadn't bought a big house. He'd grown up in a huge old place with more rooms than the family could use. This was a modest house. Granted, it was still bigger than he needed, living alone, but he loved the old place, with its wood-paneled staircase and tall ceilings. He couldn't help wondering what Greg would think of it with his architect's eye. The grand dame had style, and that was what had attracted him to her. He'd seen size over substance in many facets of his life, and that wasn't what he wanted.

After placing his things in the kitchen, he settled in what he used as a family room and turned on the television. He wondered if it was too soon to call Greg, realizing of course it was too soon, and too late in the evening. He placed the card with his phone on the coffee table so he'd remember to call the following afternoon. He didn't want to appear needy, even if he was anxious to see the man again.

His phone rang at almost eleven.

"How was the party?" his friend Skip asked, sounding a bit toasted. "You're missing all the fun you could be having here."

"Yeah, let me see. You've been to one club and are on your way to another. You can't walk a straight line, and in a couple hours you won't be able to stand up. One of the guys you're with will either drag you home or you'll end up in the bed of some guy you've never met before, wondering how in the hell you got there."

"You say that like it's a bad thing," Skip quipped. "At least I'm having fun and not hiding away in the frozen north." He began to giggle. "One of the dancers just stood in the doorway and waved at me"—another giggle—"and it wasn't his hand," Skip sang. "You can't tell me they have guys like this in whatever hell you moved to."

Tom settled on the sofa. Skip was just getting started, and he could talk for hours. It was the one thing he was really good at. "No, I doubt there are go-go boys in Marquette. Not that it matters, because there are really handsome guys here. They get their muscles from real work, not sitting in an office all day and then going to the gym and getting pharmaceutical help."

"Blah, blah, blah," Skip said. "I don't understand how you could leave New York, with everything it has, for… that place."

"I've been here almost two years. You'd think you'd be used to it by now. Whenever we talk, you tell me about all these clubs. I've never been to most of them because they opened after I left." Tom got comfortable and closed his eyes. "It's quiet here and I can think. I'm making friends, and not just the kind who want to hang around me for my money."

"I never did that," Skip said indignantly.

"Of course not, but most of the other guys I dated did. Remember Romeo?" Tom challenged.

"Yeah. I saw him a few weeks ago. He's not as cute as he used to be. But he's still pulling that same 'I need a big strong man to help me' act. I can't believe you fell for that crap." Skip giggled again, and Tom heard music thumping in the background. Skip must have been approaching whatever club he'd been walking to.

"If I remember, you thought he was a nice guy, and we didn't know it was all part of his bit until he started asking for money."

"True," Skip said.

The music in the background was louder now. "I take it you're at the next club. Go have fun and I'll talk to you later," Tom said. Skip said good-bye, and they hung up. Tom placed the phone on the table and stared up at the ceiling for a while. Then he went upstairs.

CHAPTER *Three*

A WEEK later, Greg got ready for his date. Tom had said they were going for a nice dinner, and he'd been looking forward to it for days. He was dressed, ready, and nervous. "Davey, Ken and Patrick will be here soon to pick you up. Are your things packed?"

"I'm all set, Dad," Davey said.

"You've got pajamas and extra shoes?"

"Yes."

"Toothbrush as well as your extra glasses?" Greg asked. "And your phone?"

"Yes. I got everything you put on the list." Davey set his small suitcase by the door and looked out the front window. "They're here," he said excitedly and raced for the front door, knocking the coffee table as he passed it.

Davey didn't stop, but Greg knew in his heart that Davey hadn't even seen it. He wanted to pass it off as him being in a hurry, but Davey had been doing that for weeks and Greg couldn't ignore it anymore. Jerry had said he should think about having Davey enrolled in classes for the blind, so they could start teaching him the skills he'd need to know, but Greg had been resisting, hoping for a miracle that obviously wasn't going to come. Davey opened the door, and Greg pushed his momentary worry from his mind. There was nothing he could do about it at the moment.

Ken and Patrick came inside. Davey hugged them both and immediately whisked Hanna to the back of the house to show her something he'd done on the computer. "I appreciate you taking him for the night."

"It's no problem," Ken said. "We have the room, and they get along so well. Actually, I was wondering if you'd mind if I painted Davey. I'd like to use him in a series I'm doing."

"If it's okay with Davey, it's fine with me," Greg said with a smile.

"The concept is just coming to me, but if he's willing, I'll start with some sketches," Ken said as Davey and Hanna came back in the room.

"I don't have an objection." Greg turned to Davey. "Uncle Ken would like to include you in one of his paintings, if that's okay with you."

Davey turned to Hanna, who smiled in return. "Daddy has painted me a bunch of times. He did some when I was sick and then afterwards too."

"Would you paint me without my glasses?" Davey asked.

Ken smiled. "If that's what you'd like. But let me do the sketches first and you can see what you think. Okay?"

Davey nodded and gave Greg a hug. Then he picked up his suitcase. Greg held the door and watched as the four of them walked out to Ken's car. He waved, and Davey waved back before getting in the car. Greg watched as they drove away, and then he closed the door. He checked his watch. Tom was due in ten minutes. Greg hurried up the stairs and checked how he looked in the full-length mirror in his bedroom before going back downstairs to wait.

Tom knocked on the door a few minutes later. Greg opened it and welcomed him inside. Tom immediately looked around. "This is really nice. Did you design it?"

"No. The house was here, but I remodeled the inside. It was a normal ranch house, but I opened it up to create the larger interior space and then added the wing with the family room. There were so many houses like this built in the fifties, sixties, and seventies, and they're very cookie-cutter. I wanted to show that you could take one of these rather bland houses and turn it into something special," Greg explained as he showed Tom around. "There are defined spaces, but they're defined by furniture and the beams rather than walls, which makes everything appear larger."

"This is way cool," Tom said, "and I love the way you used the tiger maple throughout. It unifies the various spaces and makes everything cohesive."

"I debated whether I should include the kitchen in the space or not, but I'm glad I did. Davey can be doing his homework at the table while I'm making dinner, and I can see and help him."

Tom nodded as he continued looking around. "Cool," he said again, and Greg beamed. "I love the antique chandelier in the dining area. Everything is so simple, yet elegant. I love this place."

"Thanks," Greg said. "The bedrooms are down the hall. I haven't had much done to them other than changing the hallway woodwork to match what I did in here and have the bathrooms redone. There are still some things I'd like to do, but those can come in time. The major project is done."

Greg watched Tom look around, and then they got ready to go. "Where's Davey?"

"He's at Ken and Patrick's for the night," Greg answered. He made sure he had all he needed and led the way to the door. He held it for Tom and followed him out, locking it behind him.

He followed Tom out to his dark-blue BMW. The car was gorgeous, and Greg felt a slight pang of envy. "I've always wanted one of these." He'd thought about buying one a few years earlier, but put the money in Davey's college fund instead. That was much more important than driving an expensive car.

"I really like it," Tom said. They got inside the car, and Tom backed out of the drive. "I made reservations for us. I wasn't sure what you liked to eat, so I took a chance and chose good, basic food."

Greg had been expecting someplace fancy, but Tom took them to a small restaurant just off one of the main commercial streets.

"It's really good Italian—basic, but well done." Tom parked, and they got out. "I hope this is okay."

"Of course," Greg said as he followed Tom inside. It was small, but the scent of garlic and herbs was a bit of heaven. They were shown to their table and given menus by the hostess. Greg glanced at the menu, but spent more time looking at Tom. After a few moments, he knew he'd been caught watching and blushed a little. Tom smiled and placed his menu on the table, openly looking at him.

Neither of them talked, and Greg started to wonder if they had anything to talk about. At the party they'd spent hours together without a lull in the conversation, but they'd talked mostly about Davey, and Greg didn't want to spend his date talking about his son. There had to be something. "Do you play any sports?" Greg asked.

"In college I was on the lacrosse team," Tom said with a grin. "We were a rowdy and raucous group, as you'd expect. I also did some intramural sports, like baseball and basketball, mostly because it was fun." Tom shifted slightly. "I found out pretty early on that I'm very competitive and don't like to lose. Most of the guys in lacrosse were like that. But the intramural stuff didn't feel nearly as competitive and I could sort of let that part go. It helped me focus on what was important. How about you?"

"Baseball all the way. My dream as a kid was to play pro and make it to the big leagues. It might have worked out, but other opportunities presented themselves, and I chose architecture instead."

"Do you coach or anything?" Tom asked.

The server approached, and their conversation halted while they listened to the specials. Then they each ordered a beer.

"Where were we?" Greg asked. "Oh yeah, coaching. I thought about it, but I really hate it when fathers coach their own kids. Either they end up playing favorites or are too hard on their kid. Neither is good, so I've helped out with Davey's Little League team and volunteered and stuff like that, but I don't coach."

"I always wondered if I would have the patience. I like kids, but being around fifteen or sixteen ten-year-olds is enough to try the patience of a saint," Tom said, and Greg nodded his agreement. Sometimes the noise alone could be overwhelming.

"I agree, but someone had to do it, otherwise the kids lose out. The last two years he played, Davey had great coaches. One had been coaching for years, and he was so good with the kids. Never yelled or even raised his voice. He never had to. The kids wanted to please him so badly that it was never necessary. Then Davey's last year, one of the other boys' father coached. He seemed to strike the balance really well. But there was sometimes tension. It's normal, but he was a fair man and a good coach. But Davey couldn't play the entire season. His vision got too bad."

"Did Davey enjoy playing?" Tom asked.

"He did. He was good at it. Coordinated, could catch and hit." Greg couldn't keep the pride out of his voice and a smile off his face. "I had hoped he'd be better than I was." Greg shrugged. It wasn't to be.

"Has he played anything else?" Tom asked, and just like that they were on the subject of Davey. Greg realized he'd brought it up and it was probably inevitable.

"He wanted to try out for football, but he wasn't the right build. I played when I was young, but I wasn't the right build either." Greg sipped from his water glass. "I didn't want him to play. Being physical is one thing, but that game is way too hard on young bodies. It may sound un-American, but I wanted him to take part in less dangerous sports."

"You're a father and you worry about your son," Tom said. "I know I'd be wary of letting my kid do some of the things my dad let me do."

"Did you grow up here?" Greg asked.

"Gosh, no. We lived outside Grand Rapids, and I went to Columbia for school. After college, I stayed in New York for almost four years. It was one long party. When it was time to grow up, I decided to leave New York and settle somewhere else. My parents had brought me here on vacation when I was a kid, so I looked into it and moved here a couple years ago."

The server brought their beer and a plate of bread.

"My friends think I'm crazy because they're still so into the club scene and New York night life. But I'm over it. I moved here because I wanted a home. I've had friends visit and they love it for a few days. Then the slow pace and quiet starts to get to them." Tom chuckled. "How about you?"

"I grew up outside town. My folks had a farm that they lost in the eighties. Dad borrowed too much for too many years, and in a drought year, there was no money. Everything was auctioned off, and I dreamed of being a professional baseball player. It was what kept me going and what got me to college. I got scholarships and borrowed the rest of the money. I was even scouted and got an offer." Now, he knew he'd made the right choice. But at the time it had been a hard decision.

"So you were out of school when you had Davey."

"Yeah. Like you, I came here in search of a home. In my case, it was more for Davey. As my reputation grew, I found that people would seek me out, so I didn't need to be in a huge city." Greg sipped his beer. "What surprised me was the arts and sense of community here."

"The university helps with that somewhat, but so do people like Ken, who is a nationally known artist and helped put this area on the map," Tom said.

There was a glint in Tom's eyes, and Greg wondered what it meant. He was about to ask when their server brought their entrees, and Greg turned his attention to food. His pesto smelled amazing, and his stomach rumbled in anticipation.

"Gosh," Greg said after taking the first bite. He tried not to roll his eyes and failed.

"I know. After all that time in New York with great Italian food, this place beats them all. I asked once, and they said they use their great-grandmother's recipes. Their sauces are all made from scratch, and they only use the best ingredients."

"It shows," Greg agreed. His phone vibrated in his pocket and then stopped right away, indicating a text message. He pulled out his phone and saw that Davey was having a good time. He sent him a quick response and then placed the phone upside down on the table. "Just Davey saying he's having fun. Ken asked if he could use Davey in one of his paintings." The phone buzzed again. "Ken is sketching him."

"That's cool," Tom said.

"Davey asked him to not include his glasses. He's worn them for a few years, but the ones he has now are so thick. He hates them, but can't see much at all without them." The phone vibrated a few more times, and then Greg sent Davey a message to have a good time and the messages stopped. "I'm not sure what to talk about," Greg confessed.

"How about sex?" Tom asked, and Greg nearly sprayed beer over the table. "See, that's always a subject everyone has lots to say about. I don't know about you, but I'm all for it."

Greg stared slack-jawed, and then Tom grinned.

"When you're at a loss for words, say something outrageous; it's guaranteed to start a conversation. Either that, or the other person moves away, leaving room for someone more interesting. At least that generally works at parties. Although there was that one time when I did that and the guy talked right back, didn't miss a beat. The problem was he talked and talked my ear off the rest of the evening about replacement toner cartridges, if you can believe that. Seems he'd developed some process to reuse old ones. Man was as dull as dirt."

Greg's eyes widened. "I take it you're rarely at a loss for words."

"Not if I can help it. Growing up the way I did, making small talk was an art. I can spend hours talking to just about anyone about anything and actually say nothing whatsoever."

"Is that what you're doing now?"

"Oh, gosh, no." Tom winked. "It's just one of my skills."

"You said you managed money for a living," Greg said.

"Yes. My family has a charitable foundation, and I'm in charge of managing the money and distributing the proceeds to worthy organizations." Tom stopped abruptly and became enamored with his food.

Greg knew there was something he was trying to avoid saying. He waited.

"I try to avoid certain subjects, not because I'm ashamed, but because they make getting to know someone difficult."

"You have money," Greg supplied with a shrug. "I knew that already, based upon the people your family knew and the way you grew up. Most people don't have nannies."

"Yeah, well, the last person I dated only wanted me for my money," Tom said.

Greg put down his fork. "It doesn't matter to me what you have or don't have. I didn't have much even before we lost the farm, but my folks loved us and spent their time and energy making each of us kids feel important and cared for. That's what I try to do with Davey. I have a better life than my parents had, and I hope Davey will have a better life than I do, but money is only part of the answer. So whatever you have is yours and you can keep it. I don't want or need it."

"Okay, then," Tom said.

"Sorry, I didn't mean to come off sounding like a prick. I'm not here because of what you have. If I didn't like you, I wouldn't spend time with you. And for the record, I'm not rich, but I do okay, and Davey and I have a good life."

"I understand," Tom said. "Money is a strange subject. We can talk about all kind of other topics, including sex and religion, but money makes everyone nervous and uptight."

"Yeah, I suppose," Greg said. "So you've really had guys date you for your money?"

"Yeah. One guy was so good at the act it took me months to figure it out. He'd used my name all over New York to get people to extend him credit. They thought I'd pay his bills, and he let them think that. I had people coming to me for months trying to get paid. Stupid jerk. One thing my grandfather always told me was never to pay anyone else's bills and never to loan money to family or friends. 'Especially family,' Grandpa always added at the end."

Greg returned to his dinner. "He sounds like a hoot."

"He was. Grandpa was one smart cookie. He started the family grocery business from nothing, and now there are stores all over the country under a number of names. He worked almost every day of his life, and so did my grandma. All their kids worked in the stores too. Grandpa made them learn the business. I worked there as well, but stopped when I went away to college.

"People were always in awe of my grandfather. He was a big man and commanded attention in every room he entered. But to me he was just Grandpa, the man who used to take me on fishing trips and camping in the summer. He did with the other grandkids as well, but he and I always had this special bond. When I was young, he was more important to me than my folks." Tom's expression turned far away. "He died when I was fourteen. So, yeah, you're right, the important things in life don't come from money, and I'd give every cent if I could have him back."

"I know exactly what you mean," Greg said, thinking of Davey.

"I really get that. But it changes things, and I want people to like me for me, that's all," Tom said.

Greg reached across the table and touched Tom's hand. "I like you for you." He made small circles with his thumb on the back of Tom's hand. "This is nice."

Tom nodded, and they grew quiet. Unlike earlier, Greg didn't wonder what they should talk about or what would come next.

They both began eating again, only now they kept sharing looks, glances, and smiles across the table. It truly felt like being a teenager again, only now it was the good parts, the excitement and energy of something new with possibilities stretching out to be explored. Both of them declined dessert, and the server brought the check. Greg reached for it, but Tom took it first.

"You can treat next time."

The thought of a next time with Tom brought a smile to his face. Greg hoped he didn't look too goofy. Tom paid and signed the receipt. Then they stood and left the restaurant. They walked to the car in the early summer night. A week earlier, the evenings had been unusually warm; now they held a slight chill. Greg wished he'd brought a light jacket, but once in the car he was warm enough. Tom didn't start the engine, and Greg turned to see what he was doing. The leather seats crunched slightly as Tom moved closer, slowly sliding his hand around the back of Greg's neck. The touch was gentle and soft, guiding, coaxing, and Greg moved into it. Their lips touched, and Greg nearly pulled away. He'd been kissed before, but it'd never been accompanied by a zing of electricity. He didn't recognize it at first. Tom seemed to, because he deepened the kiss, shifting his weight slightly and pressing against Greg.

When they broke apart, Greg gasped for air and blinked a few times, taking a second to make sure he hadn't imagined what had just happened. "Wow," Greg mouthed, and Tom smiled.

"You can say that again," Tom whispered. A couple walked by the car, breaking the spell. Tom started the engine and pulled out of the parking lot.

After a few minutes, Greg got a pretty good idea where they were going. Tom turned into the entrance of one of the parks and pulled to a stop at the edge of a bluff. Ahead of them, Lake Superior sparkled with the light of a million stars and the nearly full moon. The lake almost never looked like that, but tonight, instead of extreme northern Michigan, they could have been floating on the Caribbean.

"This is one of my favorite spots. When the lake is stormy, the waves sometimes spray the car, but on a night like this...." Tom's words floated away as he opened his seat belt and moved closer for another kiss.

Afterward, Greg leaned back in his seat, breathless, energy thrumming through him from head to toe. Tom held his hand, and they sat silently for a while, watching the light dance on the waves.

Their quiet interlude was broken when Greg's phone buzzed in his pocket. He tried to ignore it at first, thinking it was a message, but it continued, and he shifted on the seat, fishing out his phone. "It's Ken," he told Tom and then answered the call.

"Greg, I think you need to get here as soon as you can," Ken told him.

"Is there a problem?" he asked automatically.

"Yes. You need to get here."

Greg's heart raced and he relayed the message to Tom, who started the engine. Greg fumbled to put on his seat belt as Tom drove quickly out of the park and to the main highway toward Pleasanton.

"Is Davey okay?" Greg asked Ken.

"I don't know. Something is definitely wrong. We're keeping him quiet and settled, but he fell and hit his head," Ken said.

"Okay. We're on our way," Greg said, the phone shaking against his ear. "It should be about ten minutes."

"We'll be watching for you," Ken said. He hung up and Greg set down the phone.

"They said Davey fell and hit his head. They're keeping him quiet, but something is most definitely wrong. I can tell Ken is avoiding telling me something over the phone." Greg's imagination raced in a million directions.

"Have they called an ambulance?" Tom asked.

"I don't know; I didn't think to ask," Greg said, trembling in the seat.

"They would have told you," Tom said, most likely trying to be reassuring.

Greg felt the car speed up, and they flew down the highway. Greg willed the car to go even faster and hoped they wouldn't be stopped by a cop.

In record time, they pulled up in front of Ken and Patrick's house. Tom parked right out front. Greg got out of the car almost before it had come to a complete stop and hurried toward the front door. He knew Tom was right behind him, but didn't turn around to look.

The front door of the house opened, and Patrick stood off to the side to let him in. Davey sat on the sofa with Hanna hugging him. He had his hands over his eyes, crying and rocking back and forth.

"He's been like this since just before we called. I've tried to get him to talk to me, but I get nothing," Ken whispered.

Greg hurried closer. "Davey," he said, his throat constricting in fear. "What is it?"

Davey stood but then didn't move. Greg hurried to him, hugging Davey close.

"It's gone, Dad," he said. "It's gone." Davey began to cry, and the rest of his words were mumbled and not understandable.

Greg knew Davey was trying to speak, but nothing was coming out. "What's gone, Davey? Take a deep breath and tell me what's wrong."

"Daddy, I can't see anymore," Davey said and then held him tight, burying his head against Greg's chest.

Greg stroked Davey's hair and felt his own eyes fill with tears. "What happened?" he asked as calmly as he could. He still held Davey and did his best to comfort him.

"We were in the family room. He got up and stumbled over the coffee table," Hanna explained. "When he got back up, he turned around and got upset. We got him in here." She was nearly as upset as Davey.

"Davey, it's going to be all right. I'll call the doctor and we'll see what he says," Greg soothed, as calmly as his trembling heart would allow.

Patrick came forward and cradled Davey in his arms. Greg stepped back and fished Jerry's number from his wallet. He left a message with the answering service and got a call from Jerry back a few minutes later. Greg explained what had happened.

"All right. I want you to bring him into the office first thing Monday morning. Can he see anything at all?" Jerry asked.

"Davey," Greg said, and Davey turned toward his voice. "Can you see anything at all?"

"Only brightness," he croaked, and Patrick held Davey once again.

Greg relayed the message to the doctor.

"Okay. We've seen this before. His vision stabilizes for a month or two and then deteriorates again. We've known this day was coming. I was just hoping he'd have more time."

"We all were. Is there any reason to take him to the hospital?"

"You can. I'll meet you there if you like. They'll probably admit him, and we'll order the tests, but I can do the same thing on Monday and he'll be home with you for the rest of the weekend. I'll support whatever you decide." Jerry waited. "On second thought, bring him into the office at nine tomorrow morning. Sunday or not, I'll meet you there."

"Thank you." Greg wasn't interested in having Davey in the hospital—keeping things as normal as possible was probably better. "We'll see you then." Greg hung up and looked around the room, trying to catch his breath. He wondered what he was going to do. What Davey was going to do. Yes, they'd both known this day was coming, but he'd wanted Davey to have as normal a life as possible. He still wanted that, but putting things off now wouldn't help anyone. They'd lived on hope and prayers for months, and now both had run out. "Davey," Greg said gently. "We're going to go home now."

Davey nodded but didn't move away from Patrick.

"I'll get his stuff," Hanna said and hurried away.

"It's really going to be okay. The doctor is going to see you tomorrow morning, and we'll figure out what to do from there." He took Davey's hand and Davey moved away from Patrick. Greg put his arm around his son's shoulders and held him close. He kept wondering how it must feel for him to no longer be able to see. Part of Davey's world had just flicked off like a switch. Hanna returned with Davey's suitcase, and Greg took it from her.

"Please let us know what you find out," Ken said, standing next to Patrick, who nodded.

"Of course," Greg said. "I'm sorry about all this," he whispered, not sure what else to say.

"Nothing to be sorry for," Ken said.

They were clearly upset and concerned. Greg moved toward the door, guiding Davey, who felt his way in front of him. "It's all right. I have you," Greg crooned gently. "Take a single step down. There are three more ahead of you." He guided Davey down the stairs and along the walk out to the car. Tom followed behind them and got into the driver's seat.

Greg climbed into the backseat with Davey, and they rode in near silence toward home. "I really appreciate this, Tom," Greg said.

Tom reached back with one hand and gently touched Greg's leg. "It's perfectly fine. I understand."

Tom didn't sound the same, and Greg figured after this kind of end to their date…. Tom didn't speak much on the drive. He pulled into the driveway and hurried around to help them out of the backseat.

"Thank you for everything," Greg said formally. From Tom's silence and discomfort, Greg didn't think he would be hearing from him again. They might have gotten along well, but this didn't bode well for any future relationship.

"Do you need some help?"

"No. We'll be fine. I'm going to get him inside and up to bed. I have an idea that tomorrow is going to be very hectic."

"We'll talk soon, then," Tom said.

"Sure," Greg answered and then turned, guiding Davey toward the house. He heard Tom pull away, his headlights panning across the yard. He barely had the time or energy to think that was probably the last time he'd ever see him.

Greg got them inside and helped Davey up the stairs to his room. Everything took longer, and once he had Davey in his pajamas, he got his teeth brushed and then in bed. He sat with Davey and talked to him softly until he fell asleep. Then Greg went to his own room and got ready for bed. Not that he expected to be able to sleep very much. He was worried about Davey, even though he already knew the answers. All the possibilities ran through his head over and over. In the early morning hours, when he was still staring at the ceiling, he began to wonder about Tom and realized he was going to miss him. Greg had really liked him, but guys willing to step into a family like his were hard to come by, let alone guys who were willing to be a part of a family with a blind child. No matter what Tom might have said, that was a lot to expect, and Greg had heard enough in Tom's voice. The date had gone well and they'd hit it off, but the end of the evening had most likely signaled the end of that possible relationship.

CHAPTER
Four

FOR MORE than a week, Tom wondered if things were all right with Greg and Davey. He'd tried calling, but didn't get an answer. He knew he should probably have left a message, but if they were busy, he didn't want to butt in. He also figured if Greg was too busy and didn't want to speak to him right now, he wasn't going to intrude. So as he pulled up to Ken and Patrick's, he hoped to get the skinny on what was happening.

Tom headed up the walk and rang the doorbell. He'd said he'd probably drop by, but they hadn't set a definite time. The door opened.

"Come on in," Ken said, motioning him inside. Tom stepped into the living room and saw Howard and Gordy sitting on Ken's sofa, with Patrick in one of the chairs. They all stood, and he shook hands with each of them. "You remember Howard and Gordy from the party."

"Of course," Tom said, taking the offered chair. "I was wondering if you knew how Davey was doing."

Ken looked surprised. "You haven't heard?"

Tom shook his head. "I tried calling but got no answer, and I didn't want to intrude. I suspect things are tough right now."

"His sight is largely gone and there isn't anything that can be done," Ken said. "He can see some light sometimes, but basically he's blind now."

"They've been by to talk to me once, and I think they're both trying to figure out how to get on with life. But that takes time, which they haven't had yet. Greg is talking about getting Davey a dog like Token, but I doubt they'll consider him at this stage. He needs to figure out how to do basic things without his sight before they'll place him with a service dog. But it's great to see the support Greg is giving Davey." Howard reached down and lightly touched his dog's head before standing up. "We should probably go so you can talk."

"Please don't go on my account." Tom cleared his throat. "This was a rather fortunate turn of events, because part of what I wanted to talk to Ken and Patrick about was how to get in touch with you."

"Me?" he asked, lowering himself back down.

"Yeah. I was listening to the radio a few days ago, and I heard a story that made me think of you and Davey. I've done some research and I need some advice."

"What was the story about?"

"Beep baseball," Tom said. "Baseball for the blind. Greg said Davey used to play ball and that he was good at it, but couldn't play anymore because of his sight. I looked it up and read about it. The ball makes a beeping sound, and so do the bases. Instead of catching the ball and throwing it, the runner is safe if they make it to first base before the fielders pick up the ball. It really sounded interesting, and I was wondering if you could help."

"Because I'm blind?" Howard asked.

"Well, yeah," Tom said. "It sounded interesting, and baseball is something Davey did before he began losing his sight. I know adjusting is going to be hard, so I thought this might give him back something he used to do. It could also help him adjust to being blind. He'll have to learn to follow sounds rather than using his eyes. This could give him a way to help learn that. I checked and there's nothing like this in the area, so I was thinking of trying to put something together, but I can't do it alone. There's also no use trying if people aren't interested."

"What do you need me to do? Help raise money or something?"

"We don't need money. I can get that from my family's foundation. But you must have contacts in the area—organizations that work with the blind, support groups? I need to get the word out for blind players and sighted helpers. I can put some feelers out to other organizations to see if we can get help from people who have already set this up elsewhere."

"You're really serious about this, aren't you?" Howard asked.

"Yes. I can't get over the sight of Davey holding his father. He must have been thinking his life was over, but it isn't. It doesn't have to be. But it will take someone or something to show him he can do some of the things he did before."

"Okay," Howard said. "I'll contact the groups I'm aware of and see if they'll help discern if there's any interest."

"So how does this work?" Gordy asked. "I mean, Howard can't throw or catch to save his life."

"The pitchers are sighted and on the hitter's team. Certain functions are done by the sighted, like helping batters to the plate. The rules are adjusted, and there are only three bases, first, third, and home. The balls beep, and the bases are upright and buzz. The sounds are different. The equipment can be ordered online. It's costly, but that isn't an issue. I can get what we need as far as equipment. What I can't get are people who might be interested in playing."

"You'll also need a place to play," Gordy said.

Tom nodded. "That shouldn't be a problem. The county has parks with open space. It doesn't seem to need an actual baseball diamond because the bases are different. All we really need is an open space that's level and free of holes and hazards. I'm sure we can get the county to pony up something."

"They can be pretty stubborn," Ken said.

"Yeah, but are they going to go on record as being against the blind?" Tom smiled. "Not likely. And even if they do, I can bring pressure like they've never seen." Tom was fairly sure of that.

"Okay. I think you've won all of us over. Now you've got the hard part to do: convincing Greg and Davey."

"What's to convince?" Tom asked, looking at everyone.

It was Howard who answered. "I can tell you from experience that the most protective parent on the planet is the one with a blind child. Mine were protective for years. I didn't find any freedom in my own life until I went to college, and even then my folks tried to figure out how they could go with me. No, getting past Greg is going to be like getting into Fort Knox. Besides, Davey might not be interested in playing. I was born blind, so I never had to adjust to losing my sight. Davey is making that adjustment and that is going to be huge for him."

"Oh," Tom said. "I was so excited about the idea I hadn't thought of that."

"We're not saying you shouldn't approach them," Gordy said, and when Tom looked at Patrick, he was smiling and nodding. "I think it's a great idea, and I'll help coach or whatever you need me to do." Gordy took Howard's hand. "I think it would be good for this one to learn to play as well."

"You do?" Howard asked skeptically and sounding a little put out.

"Exercise in a controlled environment, where you can do the things you were never able to as a kid, would be good. We listen to baseball in the car all the time because I enjoy it. Now you'd have the chance to play yourself." Gordy nudged Howard's shoulder, then leaned in and whispered something in Howard's ear. Howard nudged Gordy back.

"Okay. I'll help too," Howard agreed.

"We wanna help," Hanna added, standing in the doorway with Sophia.

"Excellent," Tom said. "Then we have a plan. We'll get the word out and arrange for permission. The equipment can be ordered online, and I'll arrange that as soon as I can."

They talked of general topics for a while, and then Tom got up to leave. He received a hug from everyone, especially Patrick, and then left the house. He drove back toward Marquette and without much thought, turned down Greg's street. The garage door was closed and he didn't see a car out front, but he pulled into the drive anyway, then marched up to the front door and rang the bell.

"I'll get it," he heard Davey say, and then he waited. The door didn't open, and Tom became concerned. He tried the knob and pushed the door open, peering inside. Davey stood in the middle of the living room, stock-still. "Dad!" he yelled. A door closed and Greg hurried into the room, fastening his belt. "I don't know where I am."

"It's okay," Greg said and helped Davey to the sofa.

"Sorry," Tom said once Greg had Davey settled.

"It's okay," Greg said.

"I tried calling a few times, but I knew you were busy and I didn't want to bother you," Tom explained, swallowing hard. Greg looked haggard, like he hadn't slept since Tom had seen him last, and Davey was a nervous wreck. "How are you getting on, Davey?"

He shrugged. "I can't see anything and I keep getting lost." He gripped the edge of the sofa cushion in his fist. "I can't do anything, and every time I move, I can't remember where I am or how to get where I want to go. I hate it." He pounded the sofa cushion and stomped his feet.

Greg immediately sat next to him and tried to provide comfort, but it wasn't working. Tom looked around the room and then motioned to Greg, who got up and walked over to where he stood. "I don't know much about these kinds of things, but have you paced off the room with him?"

"He can't see," Greg snapped.

Tom persisted. "I've been reading a lot in the last few days, and if he's going to become familiar with his home, then he needs to be shown it in a new way, one he can understand. "Davey, would you stand up for me?" He did, but then didn't move. "What's right in front of you?"

"The coffee table?" Davey answered, reaching out to touch it.

"Now, if you take two small steps to the left and then two small steps forward you should be in front of the chair. Can you do that?" Tom wasn't sure he should take charge like this, but everything he'd read said Davey needed to understand the spaces around him from his new perspective.

Davey moved slowly. "Is this right?"

"Feel behind you," Tom said with a smile. "That's the arm of the chair… and there you have the second arm, now, sit down." Davey did. "Do you remember where the furniture was in the house and what the areas looked like?" Davey nodded. "Then feel your way from your chair to the dining table. I'll instruct you if you need it. We're both here to help, but we aren't going to guide you. Is that okay?"

Davey smiled at him and nodded. When Tom looked at Greg he expected to see anger, but instead saw relief. Tom reached for Greg's hand and squeezed it slightly.

"Thank you," Greg mouthed.

"Tell me what's next to the chair you're sitting in?"

"There's a table with a lamp on it, and then next to that is another sofa. Then an opening that I can use to get to the dining area."

"Okay. Then why don't you stand up and carefully make your way to the sofa, then along it until you're out of the seating area. The distance between the sofa and coffee table is about a foot and a half. Use your hands if you need to, but give it a try," Tom encouraged.

Davey hesitated.

"I know you can do it," Greg said and came around to the coffee table, clearing it of anything Davey could knock over. He put those things away. "You're doing great. The sofa is right alongside you and there's nothing in front of it. The coffee table is on your right and you're just fine." Greg actually smiled, and it got larger as Davey reached the edge of the sofa. Tom remained quiet, since Greg seemed to have taken over. "The table is five small steps in front of you."

Davey took the steps, searching in front of him with his hands until he felt the back of one of the chairs. He turned and grinned at them.

"See? You did it," Tom said. "From where you're standing, the kitchen is on your left. If you turned and walked about eight small steps, you'd be in line with the entrance. If you turned right and took eight or nine steps, you'd be at the entrance to the hall to the bedrooms."

"Do you want to keep going?" Greg asked.

"Yeah," Davey said, sounding relieved.

"Then where do you want to go? You're in the center of the open part of the house. There's a column back slightly and a few steps to the right. Why don't you try to find it? That way you can use that as a marker."

Davey moved and reached the post, then felt up and down it.

"Why don't you tell us what's where," Tom suggested. "Picture the room in your mind and tell us where you are and what's in each direction."

Davey was quiet, and Tom thought maybe he'd pushed for too much too soon.

"The one sofa is right there." Davey took a few steps and reached it. "The coffee table, chair, and other sofa are there. Behind me is the dining room table, with the kitchen over there." He pointed in the right direction. "The fireplace is there, and the front door should be that way."

"Very good," Greg said. "Do you think you can make it to your bedroom from here?"

"I'll try," Davey said. Tom sat down and watched as Greg worked with Davey, opening his dark world up for him. Once Davey reached the door to his bedroom, he let out a small whoop. "I'm going to go to the bathroom."

"Do you need me?" Greg asked, but Davey had already reached the door and was going inside. "That was great," Greg told Tom once Davey closed the bathroom door. Then he paused, as if he wasn't sure what to say. "I saw you'd called, but I... I wasn't sure you'd want to see me again. And I've been so busy this past week with appointments and...."

"I stopped by to see how you and Davey were doing." Tom suddenly felt uncomfortable. "I didn't mean to interrupt or barge in on you. I was just concerned and wanted to make sure you were both all right."

"No," Greg said more lightly, "I'm glad you came. We've been wallowing for most of the week. Davey's doctor sent us to a specialist, but there isn't any hope. He's seen every doctor who might help within hundreds of miles, not that there are many, but they all said the same thing."

"Okay," Tom said. "Then we need to help Davey adjust to being blind. He needs to be able to find his way around the house and he needs to learn to read Braille. Have you enrolled him in classes?"

"Yes. He starts next week," Greg answered. "He isn't thrilled about it."

"Of course not, because he's still hoping for that miracle, just like you were. But he needs help and he needs to learn." God, he sounded preachy. Tom quieted. "I came up with an idea that Davey might like, but I wanted to talk about it with you first. I heard a story and read online about beep baseball. It's for the blind. You said Davey used to play, and I thought if we could arrange it, that he might like to join."

Greg shook his head. "How can Davey catch a ball?" He sounded skeptical.

"He doesn't. The rules are different. The ball beeps, and so do the bases. There are roles for sighted people, but the players are visually impaired. I thought if you were interested, I'd get a set of equipment and we could see if Davey likes it. He's going to have to learn to follow sounds, and since he can already play baseball, this might be a transitional activity for him. Howard and Gordy are going to put the word out. I don't know if we'll get enough players for a team, but it might be fun just as an activity." Tom had originally thought of trying to set up actual games, but maybe that wasn't necessary. Maybe just playing and allowing Davey to hit and try to field the ball would help him. If he were the only blind player, it wouldn't matter, as long as he got something out of it. "I bet we could get Howard to play too."

"I don't know," Greg said. "Running and hitting, with balls coming at him, beeping or not. What if he gets hurt?"

Tom had been warned and he'd thought about that the entire ride over. "There would be plenty of supervision, including you. Maybe you could pitch," he suggested. "You used to play, so you have to have a good throwing arm. It doesn't have to be fast or anything. The whole point is to make it fun."

"Make what fun?" Davey asked, standing outside the bathroom door. His shirt was half tucked in and there was toilet paper on his shoe.

"Nothing, Davey," Greg said hastily. "It's nothing."

Davey felt along the walls as he made his way toward where Greg was standing. He nearly stumbled multiple times. Greg moved toward him.

"Don't help me, Dad!" Davey yelled. "I want to do this. I'm not a baby, and I want to know what you were talking about." He reached the sofa and half sat, half tripped onto its cushions. "Make what fun?"

"Davey, it's been a hard week and you're upset," Greg said quietly.

"Of course I'm upset, Daddy. I'm blind. I want to play with my friends, but I can't." Davey sat up and began rocking back and forth, occasionally punching the cushions. "I want... I want...," Davey kept chanting over and over.

Tom figured he didn't have the words to explain what he wanted, but it was clear as day to Tom. He wanted his old life back, which was something he could never have. His life, and for that matter, Greg's life, had changed forever.

"Davey," Greg whispered and sat next to his son, trying to comfort him, but it didn't work. After a while, Davey began pummeling his dad with shallow blows. "Calm down."

Davey kept struggling and hitting. The blows had no power other than to wound Greg's spirit. Tom could see the hurt building with each frustrated blow.

"Davey," Tom said firmly, and Davey paused. "You shouldn't hit your father."

Davey looked in Tom's direction and then seemed to understand what he'd been doing. Tears welled in his eyes, and then Davey gripped his dad tight, sobbing on his shoulder.

"It's okay," Greg soothed. "You didn't hurt me." Greg held Davey, and Tom got ready to go. The two of them had to work things out. He didn't have a place here and he'd most likely overstayed his welcome and overstepped his bounds already.

"Tom was just telling me about a version of baseball for people who can't see very well," Greg said. "The ball and bases make noise so you can find them. He came over to ask if you'd be interested in playing. He said Uncle Howard might play, and they're trying to find other people to play too." Greg paused and looked at him. "You don't have to play if you don't want to. No one is going to make you."

"How can I hit a ball I can't see? How can I do anything when I can't see?"

"Davey," Tom said as softly and carefully as he could. "There are people who play this game all over the country. People like you and Uncle Howard. They have fun. It isn't the same as it was before, but you can hit the ball because it beeps. So do the bases. All you have to do is follow the sound. Keep your ear on the ball."

Davey stilled and lifted his head from Greg's shoulder. He wiped his eyes and slowly shifted on the sofa, but not too far away from his dad.

"Would you like to give that a try?" Greg asked. "Like I said, you don't have to."

"Uncle Howard's going to do it?" Davey asked.

"Yes," Tom said, hoping like hell he wasn't telling a bald-faced lie. Howard hadn't exactly said he'd play, but he'd said he'd help, and that was probably good enough for now. "I'm going to order the equipment, and once it comes we can set it up and see how it works. Is that okay?"

Davey nodded. At least he seemed calmer.

Greg moved away from Davey and slowly stood up. He motioned toward the back of the living area, and Tom followed him. "Thank you. He's been like this most of the week, and I don't know what to do."

"He's grieving," Tom said.

"No one died," Greg whispered.

"His sight did. He's grieving its loss. I think it's probably normal. He's ten years old and doesn't have the words to describe all the things he's feeling, so it comes out in frustration and anger."

"How do you know all this?"

"I majored in psychology in school," Tom explained. "The money stuff came purely by accident. Help him through what he's feeling and do your best to give him a voice."

Greg nodded and looked over at Davey.

"He also needs something to occupy his time. A major sensory input is gone. He used to watch television, play video games, and things like that. Those are gone too. He's going to mourn the loss of each thing he discovers he can't do anymore. So you have to have ideas of things he *can* do. If he were older, he'd find them himself, but he's young enough that he's going to need your help."

"I can hear you," Davey called.

Greg raised his eyebrows. "Would you like to stay for dinner? I think we could both use some company."

"If you don't think I'm intruding," Tom said.

"You'd be a godsend."

Tom agreed to stay as long as he could help with dinner. "So what do you want to do, Davey?" he asked as he walked closer to where he sat. Davey shrugged. "Do you have a computer?"

"Duh."

"Davey," Greg scolded.

"It's in my room," Davey supplied with a little less attitude.

"I'll get it," Greg volunteered, and he returned with a tablet. Greg handed it to him, and Tom began searching.

"Have you ever read *The Hobbit*?" Tom asked. Davey shook his head. "Do you want to?" When Davey nodded, Tom found an audio version and bought it after Greg put in the password, then waited for it to download. He placed the tablet in Davey's hands and started the story. Then he explained where the volume control was and stepped away. Few things soothed a haggard spirit like a good story. Once Davey seemed to settle into the tale, Tom got up and left Davey alone.

"I should have thought of that," Greg said.

"I suggest you get him a good headset, because there are lots of stories available, and since you said he liked to read, he'll go through a lot of audiobooks. I'd get him an iPod or something portable and set him up with an account he can use. You'll need to help him at first. There are software products that will read the contents of the computer screen for him, but I don't think you'll need to help him for long. He'll figure out how to use computers to help himself pretty quickly."

Greg turned to watch Davey sitting on the sofa. "That's the most he's been still and quiet in days. Even when he's been sitting, he's jittery and restless."

"He's young and has a lot of energy, but doesn't know what to do with himself. Everything has changed for him in the past week. His entire world has changed. I know I keep saying that, but it's true." Tom lowered his voice. "But that doesn't mean you can give him whatever he wants. Just like you did before, you need to make sure he understands the boundaries. At some point he's going to figure out that he can try to use his condition to get what he wants, from you and from others. Maybe not right away...."

Greg inhaled deeply. "I never thought of that."

"Of course not, and I'm probably throwing a lot at you at once, but it seems the world is doing that too."

Greg looked overwhelmed, so Tom stopped his commentary. There was only so much they could comprehend in one go.

"I should start making dinner while I have the chance," Greg said. "I've been making finger food because that seems to be the easiest for Davey to eat. When I signed him up for the classes, they said they'd teach him how to use utensils and stuff like that." Greg stopped. "I never thought about it before, but Davey is going to have to relearn almost everything." He reached out for the table and steadied himself.

"It will be all right. There are people who can teach him what he needs to know. Howard can help him as well, and once Davey's able to do things for himself, his life and your life will be easier. Davey needs to be as independent as possible. I understand that Howard lived alone before he met Gordy. It can be done." Tom moved closer to Greg. "I know it seems overwhelming for you." Tom put his arm around Greg's waist. "People forget that it isn't just Davey affected by all this. Your life changed too."

"I'd do anything for Davey."

"I'm not saying you wouldn't. But the life you had where Davey was a normal kid playing sports and going to school like everyone else is gone. It's okay for you to grieve."

Greg turned to him. "I don't have time."

Tom didn't argue. Greg moved into the kitchen and began making dinner. In the quiet moments, Tom could hear the audio from Davey's story. The meal was indeed simple, with heated frozen chicken nuggets, some vegetables, and french fries cooked in the oven. "We're living on stuff like this because it's what he can eat," Greg explained. "I offered to help feed him…." Greg's tone was heartbreaking.

"Things will get better," Tom reassured him. The sadness and doubt he saw in Greg's eyes tore at Tom's heart. "The food doesn't matter. It isn't forever, and Davey will learn a whole new set of skills. Then he'll be able to do a lot of things on his own. He'll need some time, but it will happen.

"Davey, do you think you can make it to the table on your own, or do you need help?" Greg asked.

The audio stopped and Davey reached to set the tablet on the table, but seemed to change his mind. He held it and stood up, slowly making his way along the route he'd used earlier. "You don't need to carry the tablet," Greg said.

"But if I put it down, I won't be able to find it again," Davey said, clutching the tablet to his chest. Tom said nothing and lightly touched Greg on the arm. He could tell Greg was holding his breath. Tom was, as well, and they both breathed again when Davey touched the back of one of the dining chairs. He placed the tablet on the table and then pulled out the chair and made his way around until he was sitting.

"Very good, Davey," Greg said.

"Do you like the story?" Tom asked, carrying the dishes that Greg had set out to the table. Greg motioned for him to take a seat, and Tom sat.

"Yes. It's really good." Davey placed his hand on top of the tablet like he had to make sure it was still there. "Can I listen to more after dinner?"

"Yes. But first you need to eat." Greg placed a plate in front of Davey and explained where everything was.

Davey felt around and picked up one of the french fries and began to eat. He held the plate and continued eating. Tom noticed that Greg watched Davey rather than eating his own food. Tom didn't say anything and just ate his dinner. What they were eating was less important than the company. It turned out Tom was hungry, so he ate, and eventually Greg did as well.

Davey, of course, made a mess. Half of his food ended up on the table rather than his plate. He'd pick up one piece of chicken and in the process knock another off his plate. Tom ignored it, and occasionally Greg would place the food back on Davey's plate. Tom thought that might be confusing to Davey, but he kept quiet and let Greg do what he thought was best. Not that it really mattered. Davey seemed content enough, and Greg somewhat less nerved up.

By the time the meal was over, Davey had eaten most of his dinner and managed to drink a full glass of milk without spilling much. He got up, bumping the table. Tom steadied it, and they both watched Davey make his way to the sofa. He'd forgotten the tablet and began making his way back toward the table. Greg began to get up, but Tom touched his hand and smiled as Davey reached the table and began searching for the tablet. He came close twice, and finally Tom picked it up and handed it to him.

"Thank you," Davey said as he took it and began to go back the way he came.

"Do you need help restarting the book?" Tom asked. Davey reached his seat with a small sigh. Tom stood and walked over to where Davey sat, then helped him locate the buttons to restart the audiobook once again.

"It's hard," Davey said and then turned around. "I never thought about how hard stuff could be until I couldn't see it."

"That's why we're going to class, so you'll be able to do things for yourself. Tom says there's software that will read the screens to you. I'll see if we can get it on your tablet," Greg said.

"Okay." Davey smiled slightly and then settled back with his story.

Tom returned to the table and took his seat across from Greg. "I think he's going to be fine," Tom whispered. "He wants to learn and be able to get around. He only needs the instruction and skills. He'll learn fast, I'm sure."

Greg nodded. "A lot faster than I will."

"You both have support. All you have to do is be willing to ask," Tom said as he reached across the table and took Greg's hand.

"Why would you do this?" Greg asked. "For that matter, why put in all the effort to research sports and things for Davey? What do you get out of it?"

Tom was stunned, but since Greg hadn't let go of his hand, he didn't pull it back. "Why do I have to get something out of it? Can't someone be thoughtful?"

"Yes, but people rarely are," Greg said. "At least I haven't experienced it very much. Sure, I have friends, but how much can I ask of them before I don't have any friends anymore? I have to do things for myself and for Davey."

"And if someone is there to help or is willing to spend some time and effort to make Davey's and your life a little easier, or to add some fun, then that person wants something from you?" Tom challenged. He gently tugged back his hand and shook his head. "I was raised to help others. When I was born, I had everything money could buy… except my parents' attention. Luckily I had my grandfather, who spent time with me. I told you about him at the party. He came from nothing and said that with money and prosperity come responsibility."

"So Davey and I are some charity case to fulfill your sense of responsibility?" Greg challenged.

Tom looked over at Davey, grateful he had earbuds in. Tom wondered where he'd gotten them for a second, but then he shifted his attention back to Greg.

"You aren't a charity case," Tom said, standing up. "I like you and I care about Davey. He's a good kid who's going to have a tough time of it. When I heard that story about blind kids playing baseball, I thought of him, and you." Anger welled inside him. "I don't understand how you could think I'd want anything from you." He stepped back from the table. "I spent the week wondering if you were okay. Regardless of how things ended the last time we were together, I like you and I thought you liked me too. Maybe I was wrong," Tom whispered, his anger shifting to disappointment. "Hell, I was only being nice."

Tom took another step back and then headed for the front door. He wasn't sure what to think, but it figured—he always seemed to end up with the crazies or the guys who only wanted to use him. He pulled open the door and paused, deciding he'd say good-bye to Davey. When he stopped to look at Davey, he was engrossed in his story. Tom turned to leave and felt a light touch on his shoulder.

"Why?" he asked Greg.

"I…." Greg hesitated.

Tom waited for some sort of explanation.

"It's hard to explain. I'm sorry I jumped to that conclusion. I shouldn't have."

"You're damned right about that." Tom shook his head for emphasis, the hurt settling like an ache in his heart. "Freud said that sometimes a cigar is just a cigar, and sometimes a person who's willing to help is just that—someone doing something unselfishly."

"I know," Greg whispered. "I'm sorry. I shouldn't have thought that. You've been nothing but kind and thoughtful." Greg moved back, motioning for Tom to come back in, and Tom closed the door.

"What's going on?" Davey asked, taking out his earbuds.

"Nothing. Tom and I were just talking. Go back to your story." Greg kept his voice level. He motioned back toward the dining table, and Tom followed him. He wasn't sure he wanted to hear what Greg had to say. His better judgment told him to leave and cut his losses, but he sat back down.

"I told you at the party about the fight with my ex-wife," Greg began, and Tom nodded. "After I got custody, my parents offered to help. They were living nearby and offered to help me take care of Davey. It was a load off my mind and a huge help. I hadn't told them I was gay, but when Davey was about a year old, I had a conversation with them about it. They were surprised and didn't say a great deal. When we were done, I got up to get Davey, and my father stood between me and my son and said I wasn't fit to raise him." Greg paused, his voice breaking slightly. "My own father."

"My God," Tom whispered.

"They said they would help me raise Davey but only on their terms. Actually, my father did the talking, and my mother sat silently. If she disagreed, she said nothing." Greg took a deep breath and looked to where Davey sat, oblivious to this conversation. "I've never told him what they said, but I took Davey that day and told my folks no, thank you. Their help was not worth my self-respect."

"I don't understand," Tom said. "What did they want?"

"Me to live my life the way they wanted. 'There will be none of this gay crap,' my father said, and he instructed me on the way I'd live my life if I wanted their help." Greg humphed. "The funny thing was, at that time, I was just really figuring out who I was. But in that second I knew their help would come at too high a price. So I said, 'No, thanks,' took Davey, and left."

"You walked away from your parents? Just like that?"

"I didn't have a choice. They were trying to dictate who I was. The strangest part was, it wasn't until they delivered their ultimatum that I really made up my mind. I guess you could say I had a bit of an epiphany standing in front of my father. See, he's a big man, formidable, and when he stares at you, you not only see it, but feel it too. He stared at me hard, arms folded over his chest, and I stared back. Then I got Davey and left."

"So you raised him on your own?"

"Yes. My parents thawed after a while, but I never forgot the lesson of that day: help comes with a price."

"Yeah, but what if it's a price you're willing to pay?" Tom asked.

"Excuse me?" Greg said.

"What if the price demanded for someone's help is what you're willing to pay. See, I have a story about the other side of helping. I was"—Tom thought for a few seconds—"maybe nine, and on one of our Saturdays together, my grandfather took me to a place downtown where they served people free meals. Grandpa went down there sometimes, and they knew him. I don't know if they knew *who* he was, but the people who ran the place knew him. He brought a donation, filled the trunk, and it was my job to bring everything inside. Then he and I helped with the cooking. It was a long morning, and I remember being really hot without air-conditioning in the summer. Once it was ready, I helped serve the food, standing on a chair because I wasn't tall enough. I handed out rolls to the people who came through the line." Tom stopped. "What shocked me was the number of kids, no older than me, and then I nearly fell off the chair when I recognized one of the kids. He'd been at my school the year before, but had left. We'd heard rumors, but nothing more, and then there he was standing in front of me, confirming what I'd heard: his family couldn't afford the tuition any longer."

"What did you do?" Greg asked. "Did you say something to him?"

"No," Tom said. "I gave him his roll like everyone else and pretended I didn't know who he was. But Grandpa noticed. He saw the way I looked at him, and on the way home he asked what had upset me. I told him that I'd seen Billy and who he was. My grandfather just nodded and drove me home. When school started up in the fall, Billy was there in my class once again. I never asked him why I saw him at the shelter, and he never mentioned it. The next time I saw Grandpa, I asked him about it. He shrugged and pretended to know nothing about it."

"Do you really think your grandfather had anything to do with it?" Greg asked, leaning across the table

"I never gave it much thought after that," Tom said. "Billy was smart—really smart. Anyway, he and I continued on in school together, and he was eventually valedictorian of our graduating class. In his speech, he talked about perseverance and being kind to others." Tom leaned over the table. "He talked about how his father had lost his job and he'd had to leave the school. Then his family was contacted about how he'd been awarded a scholarship, and shortly after his father landed a good job with Country Foods. He'd never found out how he got the scholarship, but things turned around for him and his family. He went on to talk about how we should all share our good fortune with others. That was when I knew Grandpa had done something. I don't know what, but he was behind all of it. I remember sitting at my high school graduation with all the other students, listening to that speech. When Billy was done, everyone applauded. I did as well, but not for the same reason as the others. I was applauding my grandfather. Though he'd been dead for a number of years, he was still touching people's lives and they didn't even know it." Tom took a deep breath. "See, he did all that without anyone knowing. He didn't make a big deal out of it; he just helped and he left them their dignity. That was the example I was given growing up. I've been given a lot in my life, and I've been lucky."

"I understand, I think," Greg said. "But what did you mean by paying the price I was willing to pay?"

"You're right, Greg, that sometimes help comes with a price, and sometimes it's more than we are willing to pay. And sometimes, it's exactly what we want to pay to get exactly what we want." Tom looked deeply into Greg's eyes, willing him to understand the point he was making.

"I don't get what you're saying," Greg said.

Tom nodded and stood up, then stepped to the other side of the table. He leaned down, locking gazes with Greg, and kissed him.

Greg hesitated for a split second before responding, returning the kiss. It didn't deepen, but the energy was there like a live wire. Tom ran his hand gently over Greg's neck, dipping into the open vee of his shirt and then stopping himself. He longed to touch, and every instinct propelled him to dip deeper, to run his fingers over the small buds he'd caught glimpses of through Greg's shirt and then slide them farther down Greg's belly. He wanted to hear Greg moan softly and know it was for him.

Tom heard movement and it pulled him back to the present. He jerked his hand away and looked over at Davey, who was still engrossed in his audiobook. Granted, he couldn't see them, but he still didn't want Davey to catch him making out with his dad. Tom pulled away, pausing to look into Greg's eyes. Neither of them moved for a few seconds. Tom smiled softly and then lightly touched Greg's shoulder.

"I should go," he said, shifting things as unobtrusively as he could. He took a deep breath to calm his racing heart. "I'll call you in the next few days and let you know what's happening. I figured we could set up a trial run with Davey and Howard once the equipment arrives." He had no illusions that a date of any kind was in the near future. "I'd like to have lunch or dinner with you and Davey. Maybe we can arrange a picnic by the lake or something," he suggested, figuring it wouldn't matter if Davey was messy, and some time outdoors might be good for him.

"I think we'd like that," Greg said and took his hand. "I'll talk to you in a few days, if not before." Greg squeezed his hand, and Tom returned the small touch.

Then he walked to the sofa, touched Davey's shoulder, and said good-bye when Davey pulled out the earbuds. "I'm going to order the beep baseball equipment when I get home."

Davey stood, and to Tom's surprise, gave him a hug. "I wanna play baseball again," he whispered.

"Then you will," Tom promised. "It might not be exactly the same, but you'll play again." He returned Davey's hug and said good-bye to both of them before heading for the door. He said a final good-bye and then left the house. It had begun to rain, and he hurried to the car, unlocking it along the way.

The drive home didn't take long, but the entire time he couldn't help thinking how much easier things would be if he simply walked away and let Greg and Davey get on with their lives. They would get along just fine without him, and Lord knew his life would be simpler. Tom pulled to a stop at the light closest to his home. It was a long light, and he usually fidgeted, especially when no one was coming, but instead, this time, he remembered that kiss—warm, rich, and electric— and the hours they'd spent talking. Even tonight, with the occasional tension, they'd been able to talk to each other easily. The light changed, and he pressed the accelerator, continuing his ride home. The ball was largely in Greg's court. Tom had made an effort and had even offered an idea for them to get together again. But he wouldn't force it. As far as beep baseball was concerned, he'd definitely move forward with that, regardless of how things went with Greg. However, the rest of it was up to Greg.

Tom pulled into his drive and pressed the button to raise the garage door. He parked the car and got out, then closed the door and headed inside. As much as he wanted to remain close to Greg, it had to be Greg's choice. With his mind made up, Tom went right to his office and booted up his PC. He needed to order the equipment, and he probably had queries and proposals to review for the foundation, so he figured he might as well get some work done. It took him well into the night to get done what should have taken a few hours. Eventually he couldn't fight his wandering mind and went to bed.

CHAPTER
Five

"DAVEY," GREG said from the doorway, "it's time for you to get up." He'd noticed his son sleeping later and later.

"Is it morning?" Davey asked with a yawn.

"Yes. It's a great day, warm and sunny," Greg answered.

"Not that I can see it," Davey muttered. Greg let it slide, figuring it was a little more of his son's frustration coming out.

"I'll have breakfast ready and we can eat on the back deck. Do you...." He stopped himself from asking if Davey needed help. He had to learn to do for himself. He'd cleared the bathroom of anything sharp and had shown Davey where everything was. He'd also worked with Davey to simplify his room for easier mobility and to lessen the possibility that he could get hurt. "Call if you need me. If you tell me what clothes you want to wear, I'll lay them out on the chair for you."

"Doesn't matter," Davey mumbled before getting out of bed and feeling his way through the room and across the hall to the bathroom.

Greg put out some clothes and left the room. As he made his way to the kitchen, he pulled his phone out of his pocket and dialed. "Tom," he said brightly when his call was answered. "Is that offer of a picnic still good?"

"Sure. I have some things I need to get done. I can pick you up in two hours, though," Tom offered.

"Perfect. I... I'm looking forward to it," Greg said with a smile. "I'm getting Davey up and I'll pack a lunch."

"I'll get the lunch, if you like. You get Davey ready." The excitement in Tom's voice was contagious, and Greg felt a burst of energy he hadn't felt in a while.

"Okay. Would you mind if I called Gordy and Howard? You were right—the anger is there almost all the time. His occupational therapist says it's normal and suggested he spend some time around other blind people. Howard was the first person I thought of."

"Call them. Just let me know how many, so I know how much food to get." Tom paused for a few seconds. "I was hoping you'd call me." He truly sounded happy.

"I wasn't sure if I should. I was expecting you to call me, and when you didn't...," Greg started. This sounded way too much like a high school conversation, so he cut it off. "I'm being dumb, sorry. I'll see you in a few hours."

"Okay," Tom told him with a chuckle and disconnected.

Greg then called Howard and Gordy. Howard answered the phone, and it seemed that all of them, including Sophia, were excited about the idea of a picnic. He finalized the details and then called Tom back before going in search of Davey. He was pulling on his T-shirt, and Greg rolled his eyes. It was inside out. How Davey had managed to do that, he had no idea.

"Uncle Howard and Uncle Gordy are going with us. Sophia is going to come too. So somehow I don't think you want them to see you with your shirt inside out."

"Dad," Davey whined. Greg helped him get it off and made sure it was on right.

"It's okay to ask for help. It doesn't mean you're weak or helpless." Greg sat on the edge of the bed. "Come here," he said gently and waited for Davey to find his way over, then he guided Davey until he was sitting next to him. "There are going to be things you can do easily, some that will take more time to learn, and others, I'm sad to say, that will be impossible."

"Uncle Howard dresses himself," Davey said.

"Yeah, but don't you think he also has Uncle Gordy to help him? Being as independent as your Uncle Howard is good. Don't get me wrong. But that won't happen overnight. He's older and had more time to learn and cope with being blind. You're just learning." Greg put his arm around Davey's shoulder, tugging him close. "I'm very proud of you. You have always made me proud, and nothing can change that."

Greg lightly stroked Davey's hair. "I love you the same as I always have. Nothing has changed there."

"Would you have loved me if I had been born blind, like Uncle Howard?"

"Of course I would have. You being able to see or not wouldn't have made a difference. I love you no matter what."

Davey nodded and stayed quiet for a full minute. Greg could almost feel him thinking. "Does Mom know about me? Do you think she'll care?"

"I haven't talked to your mother in a while," Greg said. When it came to his ex-wife, Greg knew very little any longer regarding what she liked or didn't like or how she'd feel about anything. "I'll call her if you like and make sure she knows." Greg paused. "Or you can tell her. It's up to you."

Davey shook his head.

"Okay, I'll make sure she knows. Now, let's get some breakfast and then we can get ready to go."

Getting things together to leave took longer than it used to. Greg had to pack things for himself as well as Davey. He also made a much faster breakfast than he usually would on a Saturday. He was getting the last of the beach things together when Tom knocked on the door. Greg opened it, and they began loading things in the car. Once they were ready, he guided Davey out to the car. "You probably should leave your tablet here. There's going to be sand everywhere."

"I'll leave it in the car," Davey said, and Greg acquiesced. He closed the car door and hurried back to the house to lock up.

"I told Gordy where we were going. I figured we could head to the park where you took me a few weeks ago."

"Good choice," Tom said and backed out of the drive. "So, Davey, how're the classes going? Are you learning anything?"

"They're good. They said they wanted to start with basic stuff, so they're teaching me how to eat without making a mess. They also have fake rooms where they move things around so I can get used to feeling my way. That part really sucks, 'cause last time they set stuff up so I'd get trapped."

"What did you do?" Tom asked.

Greg had already heard this story.

"I was supposed to go back the way I came and find another way around. I just pushed the sofa out of the way so I could get through."

"Clever," Tom said.

"Not really," Greg supplied. "He pushed over a table they had behind the sofa and knocked over two floor lamps." Greg grinned and then broke into laughter. "You should have seen the shock on their faces. Apparently no one had done that before. Now they give him more specific instructions."

"I bet," Tom said. "Davey, there's nothing wrong with thinking outside the box. There will be times when you'll need to. But be careful you don't hurt anyone or yourself, even if you don't always do what they expect."

Harps began playing, and Greg pulled his phone out of his pocket. "It's your mother," he said to Davey and then answered the call.

"I got your message," she said snippily.

"God, Joyce, there's no need for that. I called because Davey asked me to."

"What does he need?" He could almost hear her calculating the amount in her head.

"Joyce," Greg said. "Davey can't see anymore. His vision has been failing for a while, and a few weeks ago, the last of his sight failed. He asked me to call and tell you." He heard nothing. "Joyce," Greg prompted.

"I'm here," she said more softly. "You're saying Davey, our son, is blind?"

"Yes. That's exactly what I'm saying," he clarified. "We've been to specialists, and unfortunately it's genetic." He felt Tom lightly place his hand on his leg. His heart had been racing, but he calmed quickly. She was thousands of miles away and there was no need to get upset. "We've looked into a lot of various treatments, but there are none available for what he has. The nerves have basically shut down." He turned to peek into the backseat. Of course Davey was listening to every word, and Greg regretted making this call today. But it was too late now.

"How is he taking it?" Joyce asked, choking up.

"Like a fine young man. It's taking some adjustment, but we have a friend who is blind and he's working with Davey. He's also in therapy classes to teach him how to get around and perform everyday tasks. In the fall he's going to take lessons in reading Braille. I firmly believe he's going to thrive." He'd said that as much for Davey's benefit as for Joyce's. Greg had long ago stopped worrying or caring what she thought. But Davey needed to hear that people had confidence in him. "Do you want to speak to him? We're in the car on our way to the beach to meet some friends, but we have a few minutes." He placed the phone in Davey's hands, and Davey held it to his ear. Greg turned and glanced at Tom.

"What's worrying you?" Tom whispered as they stopped at a light.

"I'm fine, Mom," Davey said. "Dad is taking good care of me. The doctor said I would have gone blind no matter what." Davey grew quiet, and Greg shifted his gaze to the back. Tom nodded and they began moving again. "I can get around the house really well now. And I'm learning to eat without making a mess." He paused for a few seconds. "That's what they do," he said, becoming agitated. He said no more and extended the phone. Greg took it.

"What was that about?"

"I can't believe you don't have the time to teach him how to eat," she spat. "What do you do with him? Leave him with a sitter or something?"

"That's enough," Greg said. "Davey asked me to tell you and I have. Other than a card on his birthday and a present at Christmas, he hasn't heard from you in two years."

"He's my son too," she began.

"Well, that's debatable," Greg said and then took a deep breath. He was not going to go into all this in the car with Tom and Davey, who looked miserable. "I'm sorry we called," Greg said and hung up. Turning to the backseat, Greg asked quietly, "What did she say?" Davey shook his head and pursed his lips. Greg knew he wasn't going to get anything out of him right away. Hopefully some fun would help soothe his hurt feelings.

A short while later they turned into the park, and Tom pulled into the last parking spot. "We're here," Tom said happily. Davey didn't move, sitting in the backseat with his arms folded over his chest.

"I wanna go home," he said quietly.

Greg ground his teeth together. He knew he should never have let her talk to Davey. Now he was upset, and that bitch of an ex-wife had stirred things up from across the country.

"We're here, and so are Uncle Howard and Uncle Gordy. Sophia is here too. So let go of whatever your mother said and have a good time. We're going to eat, and then Tom and I will take you in the water. You can't go alone, but you can go in if you want." That seemed to mollify him, and Davey searched for the door handle, opened the door, and began to get out.

"Davey," Sophia said, rushing up to him. She took him by the hand and guided him across the sand to where Howard and Gordy were already waiting. Greg watched for a few seconds as she chattered away, helping him toward the table.

"That's what he needs—someone his own age who doesn't see him as any different than anyone else," Tom said from beside him. Tom took his hand. "Come on, let's get the basket and stuff out of the trunk. I brought enough food to feed an army." Tom opened the trunk and pulled out a basket, cooler, and a bag of food. He handed Greg the basket and cooler before closing the trunk lid. Then they headed across the sand. When they reached the table, Sophia was still chattering, and Davey was talking almost as fast. It was nice to see Davey's animated personality make a reappearance.

"Let me help," Gordy said. He took the basket and then the bag.

Tom began opening things and setting everything out. It was indeed a feast, with salads, bread, spreads, crackers, dips—most of it finger food. Greg's stomach rumbled, and even Davey leaned over the table with avid interest when they said the food was ready.

"Take a seat and we can get started," Tom said. He handed out plates. Greg helped Davey get what he wanted, and Sophia sat next to him, explaining where everything was like a pro. "She's something else," Tom whispered, and Greg followed his gaze. Davey was laughing and smiling.

"After lunch, Gordy is going to take me swimming," Sophia said. "Actually, I'm going swimming, and he's going to take Uncle Howard in the water."

"I'm going too," Davey said.

"Yup," Greg agreed. He was determined that Davey do as much as possible. "Davey's a good swimmer."

"I'm not," Howard countered. "I can keep my head above the water, but I never learned very well. My parents were afraid to let me near the water, so it wasn't until I was older that I ventured into pools and things."

"I'll be with you," Gordy said softly, and Greg watched Howard lean closer to him. With those two, it was like a magnet drawing them together. Howard seemed to know where Gordy was, regardless of whether he could see him. Greg turned away, but his gaze was drawn back to them. They were happy, contented, and secure in each other. It was something to aspire to. Greg shifted his gaze to Tom and smiled slightly to himself. He wanted what Gordy and Howard had, that much he knew.

Greg swallowed hard as he watched Tom play host. He made sure everyone was served and settled before taking the seat next to him. They shared a smile, and Tom bumped his shoulder slightly, nodding toward Davey, who was eating with relative ease compared to a week earlier. He was quiet, probably concentrating on what he was doing, but Sophia chattered away, and every now and then Davey would respond.

"It's nice to see him happy," Tom whispered. "You know, it's nice to see you happy and smiling."

"There hasn't been a lot to smile about lately," Greg said. "Sorry," he added quickly. "That isn't a reflection of you, but life in general."

"You're thinking about your ex-wife, aren't you?" Tom whispered to him.

Greg nodded. He looked across the table and knew Howard had heard their little conversation. Thankfully, Davey hadn't. Greg shifted his gaze to the food in front of him. He didn't want to ruin everyone's day, especially Davey's. He seemed so happy, and Greg felt like a wet blanket.

"Can we play in the sand?" Sophia asked. "We won't go near the water."

"All right," Gordy said. "But stay where we can see you."

"I'm going to get the buckets and toys," she told Davey and then hurried to where a net bag full of stuff rested with the rest of the beach bags. Sophia lifted it and lumbered back to the table. "I'll find us a good spot and then I'll come get you," she said to Davey. She hurried away again and set the stuff on the sand.

"Davey, come around here. I want to put some sunscreen on you, and I've got your sunglasses," Greg said, and Davey made his way around the table. Greg sprayed sunscreen on Davey's legs, arms, and carefully made sure his face, ears, and the back of his neck were protected. He handed Davey his glasses, and once Sophia had received the same treatment from Gordy, she guided Davey to where she'd set down the toys.

"Greg, I might be out of bounds, but Davey seems to be doing very well," Gordy said.

"I know it's hard being the caregiver for someone who's blind," Howard said. "Gordy makes it seem easy, but I know there are a lot of things that he does just because they need to be done."

"I want to help him," Greg said.

Gordy chuckled. "Of course you do. But there are times when it seems overwhelming. Believe it or not, it's the same way for me and for Sophia. We both love Howard very much, and he's the other half of my heart, but there are times when I need some time to myself. Some time for me." Gordy threaded his fingers in Howard's. "That doesn't mean I don't love him or wish I wasn't with him. It only means that I'm human."

Greg looked at Howard, who didn't seem upset by what Gordy had said.

"I'm perfectly able to take care of most of the things in my life. But it's easy to rely on someone else when they're there. So at least one evening a week, Gordy goes out on his own, usually to one of the local sports bars for a few drinks. He meets some friends, and they yammer about whatever ball people are kicking or throwing. The important thing is it gives him an evening of his own, that's about what he likes." Howard sighed. "Things in our lives can very quickly become about me. And in your life, things are very much about Davey right now."

"You're saying I need a bar night?" Greg teased.

"Maybe," Howard quipped right back. "What I'm saying is, it's okay to feel overwhelmed and even a little angry. Hell, it's normal. You had a life that was taken away from you."

"Remember how I said Davey was grieving?"

Greg nodded.

"It's okay for you to grieve too."

"I know. And I've thought I've done a good job with Davey. I've pushed where I thought I needed to and tried to guide where I can." His thoughts went to what Joyce had said. "My ex-wife, who hasn't been part of Davey's life, accused me of not taking proper care of him. Davey asked if she knew, and she returned my call while we were in the car." He shook his head to try to banish what she'd said. "Let's talk about something else."

"The baseball equipment arrived," Tom said, like an excited teenager. "If it's nice tomorrow, I was wondering if you'd like to take Davey to one of the parks to play. Do you want to give it a try too, Howard?"

"Sure," he answered. "I have no reference for playing baseball, but it could be fun. I did contact some of the blind support organizations in the area. They were extremely interested in helping. The sight-impaired community in this area is small, but I think they'll welcome any resources. I can call them and let them know when we'll be playing next. They can help get the word out."

"Perfect. I ordered two sets of bases and multiple balls as well as some helmets. I think it will be fun. It doesn't matter if we never actually play a game. I think having the activity available will be a benefit," Tom said.

"I agree," Howard said quickly. "When did you want to meet tomorrow?"

"Say ten at Grafton Park?" Tom offered. "It won't be too hot. I was thinking we could work on hitting and running to the bases." Tom looked at him.

Greg nodded, Tom's energy and enthusiasm infectious.

"Good," Howard said with a little apprehension in his voice.

"Don't worry, I'll be there. This should be fun," Gordy said softly, patting Howard's hand. "Token can watch you too." The dog shifted slightly beneath the table, brushing Greg's leg before settling once again.

They finished the last of the lunch, and Greg helped Tom pack things away. "I brought dessert but I thought we could go in the water first."

"Davey is both scared and excited about going in the water," Greg admitted as he watched Davey digging in the sand. Sophia was building a sandcastle, and it appeared Davey was supplying her with wet sand from a nearby hole. "He's having a ball," Greg said, finally letting go of some of the tension he'd allowed to build up. He hadn't realized it was there until he took a few deep breaths and let some of it go.

"I'm going to take Howard to change," Gordy said.

"We'll watch Davey and Sofia," Tom offered.

"No digging into the chocolate cake, though," Howard warned.

"How did you know?" Tom asked.

Gordy chuckled. "Howard can smell chocolate of any kind from half a mile away, I swear." They moved away, with Howard between Gordy and Token.

"I need to get Davey a dog like that. I know he needs to learn things first, but having a dog to help him and be his constant companion would be good," Greg said, watching Davey, who had moved over to where Sophia was working, feeling his way around the castle, which was really just a pile of smoothed sand.

"Hey," Tom called and took off in Davey's direction as a group of three older boys ran down the beach. They marched right over the castle, knocking Davey backward onto the sand.

"You should watch out, baby!" one of the boys called.

Greg raced across the sand to Davey. Sophia was already helping him up, scowling at the boys.

"You meanies!" she cried at them, her hands on her hips.

"I'm okay, Dad," Davey said. "They surprised me. I heard them coming but kept expecting them to turn away."

Greg looked in the direction they'd gone and saw Tom walking back toward them, holding two boys by the arms. He marched them past and up the beach to where two ladies sat on chairs. They were too far away to hear what Tom was saying, but from the looks of it, the boys and their mothers were getting quite an earful. Greg saw Tom let the boys go and stood back as the entire party, along with the third offender, who'd worked his way back, packed their things. Tom was still scowling as he made his way back.

"They won't be bothering you again. They're gone," Tom told Davey and Sophia and then shifted his gaze. "I explained to their mothers that they had the choice of leaving or I'd call Don Marshal, the park manager, and they could be thrown out and banned for the rest of the year."

"You can do that?" Sophia asked, eyes wide.

That was exactly the question Greg had been about to ask.

"Yup," Tom said with a wry smile. "Gordy and Howard went to change to go swimming."

"I already have my suit on under my clothes," Sophia said.

Greg was grateful he'd thought to have Davey do the same thing. It would save one change of sandy clothes. Sophia hurried back to the picnic table. Gordy and Howard had returned. Greg guided Davey back.

"Could you really have had them banned from the park?" Davey asked.

"Yup," Tom said, popping the "p." "The women argued that it was a public park. I simply informed her that last year the park needed new picnic tables and bathrooms. My family's foundation helped them secure the money. I worked with the park manager, and he was grateful for my help and owes me a few favors, so having them banned from the park for bad behavior would take a phone call and nothing more. They left."

Greg sat down and guided Davey onto the bench. He helped him out of his shirt and then began spraying on more sunscreen. "I need to change, so you stay here with Uncle Howard and Uncle Gordy until I get back. I shouldn't be long, and then I'll take you in the water." Greg hurried to the bathroom and changed into his suit. When he returned, Tom was sitting next to Davey, ready to go into the water. Greg did his best not to stare. He and Tom were about the same age, but Tom didn't look like most guys in their mid to late thirties. There might have been a touch of gray in his hair, but the strength and fitness that had been hinted at under Tom's shirts was most definitely on full, mouthwatering display.

"Let's get wet," Gordy said, and their group made its way toward the water. Sophia raced ahead, wading into the edge of the water while she waited for everyone else.

"Take a few more steps and you'll be able to feel the edge of the waves," Greg said. They stepped onto the wet sand, and a few seconds later, water raced around their feet and then ran back out. "God, that's cold." Greg shivered.

"Wimp," Davey said from next to him, laughing.

"The water gets deeper just ahead," Greg said. "Do you want to go out?"

"Yeah," Davey said, inching forward. In a few steps the water went from ankle to knee depth.

Greg shivered, and Davey bent down. "If you splash me, you're on your own," Greg warned.

Sophia walked over, splashing Davey a little, and he retaliated. Within seconds, water was flying everywhere, with Greg in the middle. He released Davey, who stood still and sent water in every direction. Gordy and Howard got into the act. Greg stepped out of the water, watching Davey closely.

Tom stood next to him on the sand, still dry, laughing like a fool. "Now, that's something I never thought I'd see—a water fight between two blind guys."

Gordy had moved away, carrying Sophia along with him, leaving Davey and Howard to splash each other, laughing and grinning like fools.

Tom moved closer, and Greg felt him slide his arm around his waist. It felt good, and he closed his eyes. He'd always imagined being swept off his feet with passion and desire, but this was much quieter, calmer, and equally nice. "Maybe I should get Davey in case he falls."

Gordy joined them, carrying a squealing and laughing Sophia. "No. Let them have their fun. The waves are small, and I doubt either of them will move a step until they wear themselves out."

Token ran back and forth along the shore, playing right along with the two of them.

"Okay, Davey," Howard said. "You win."

Davey put his hands in the air, and Greg moved back into the water to help his dripping son out. "I take it you had a good time." Tom brought a towel and Greg wrapped Davey in it. The water was indeed cold, and Davey was shivering by the time Greg got him out. "Let's get you in dry clothes and then we can have dessert."

Davey nodded, shivering. Greg got the bag of dry clothes and guided Davey toward the bathrooms. Once inside, he helped Davey get dry and change into fresh clothes. Then they made their way back to the table.

"What is that?" Davey asked inhaling deeply.

"Chocolate cake from Hasper's," Tom said.

Greg's stomach rumbled. That was the premier bakery in town, and they made the best cake on earth. Tom cut and placed pieces on plates, then passed them all around. Sophia came around and sat next to Davey, explaining where the cake was and guiding him so Davey could eat. She was a godsend. Greg sat next to Tom.

"This was a great idea," Gordy commented.

"It was. The water's cold as hell, but the air is warm and it's nice to be outside," Greg said, and the adults laughed before getting down to eating.

By the time they were done, clouds had begun rolling in across the lake. Tom packed up the last of the food, then hauled things back to the car. The others packed up as well, and just before everyone got into the cars, the first drops of rain began to fall.

"If you don't like the weather, wait ten minutes—it'll change," Greg quipped. Living this close to the lake, the weather could be dicey. The big lake could generate storms even on an otherwise clear day. There were times when driving ten minutes from the lake could raise the temperature twenty degrees and be the difference between rain and sun.

"Any ideas?" Tom asked.

"Let's go back to my house. If it's not raining there, we can have a beer on the deck. Otherwise, you're welcome to hang out if you like," Greg offered. He hadn't really planned beyond their picnic.

Tom drove to the house and parked in the driveway. The rain was little more than a drizzle, but by the time they got inside, it began coming down harder. Tom brought in the basket and put the leftover food in Greg's refrigerator. Once everything was put away, Greg got a couple of beers and they settled on the sofa. Davey was in his room listening to another book, so they had the place mostly to themselves.

"The quiet is nice," Greg said softly.

"Yes. Sometimes it gets to be a bit much, though," Tom said.

"Don't you have a million friends?" Greg asked.

"I have friends in New York, but...." Tom shrugged. "I have friends here, but it isn't the same as having someone in your life." He shifted. "However, I can tell you it's better to be alone than with the wrong person, and I've spent enough time with the wrong guy that I should know." Tom placed his bottle on the coffee table without drinking. He then took the bottle from Greg's hand and set it next to his. Tom leaned closer, sliding a hand around Greg's neck, drawing them close.

Tom was an amazing kisser: firm, authoritative, and tender at the same time. There was no doubt about it, and Greg loved every second. He kissed back and felt Tom press him against the cushions. He resisted for a few seconds and then gave Tom control.

"I saw you watching me today," Tom said.

"Yeah, I was watching you," Greg admitted.

"I was watching you too," Tom said, sliding his hand under Greg's shirt. "You're a handsome man." Somehow Greg doubted that. He'd never thought of himself as handsome. But he wasn't going to argue, not now. Greg wound his arms around Tom's neck and held on as Tom kissed him once again.

"We can't do this," Greg said after a few minutes. He sat up and listened for Davey, but heard nothing.

"He's listening to a book."

Greg nodded. He knew that, but it didn't seem right to be making out on the sofa while Davey was in the next room.

"You're allowed to enjoy yourself," Tom said. "I know the past few weeks have been hard, but you don't need to make things harder on yourself." Tom moved closer. He wrapped an arm around him, but didn't push. "It's okay to be happy. You didn't do anything to cause Davey's blindness."

"The doctors said they believe it's a genetic abnormality," Greg said. "Which means he got part of whatever is wrong with him from me."

Tom scoffed and Greg scowled. "Look, we all inherit things from our parents. Some hit the genetic lottery with good looks, brains, and athletic ability, and others don't. But I can guarantee that Davey does not blame you, so you don't need to blame yourself.

Greg shook his head. "Joyce and I got along like cats and dogs for most of the time we were together. I should have known the mixture of our DNA would result in some...." He couldn't find the word right away.

"The mixture of your DNA created Davey. He's a great kid. So he's blind. There are worse things." Tom shifted closer and simply hugged him. "Do you think of Davey as flawed in some way?"

Greg thought for a second.

"He's not, any more than we're flawed for being gay. Not being able to see is part of who he is. I know it's recent, but you have to help him understand and accept that."

"But how?" Greg asked.

"By accepting it yourself and acting like it's no big deal. Treat him the way you always did. He isn't made of glass and isn't going to break. So let him find his way. You did today, and he had a ball playing in the water with Howard." Tom slowly leaned in closer. "And I'll say it again: it's okay for you to be happy too."

Greg thought Tom was going to kiss him, but he stopped.

"Do I make you happy?"

Greg curled his lips upward. "Yes," he whispered, and Tom kissed him.

CHAPTER
Six

TOM LOADED two of the bases, balls, and a couple of bats into the trunk of the BMW. It was gorgeous outside, with no hint of the rain they'd had the day before. He'd debated taking one of the other cars, but the sedan worked best for what he had to carry, so he'd decided to take that. He drove over to the park and began unloading the equipment. One of the diamonds was in use, but the other was free, so he walked over and began setting up and checking out the bases. Tom plugged in the bases, which seemed to be functioning well. He'd gotten the balls charged, too, and they seemed to be working. With everything ready, he waited for the others to arrive.

Greg pulled in a few minutes later. He and Davey got out of the car, obviously a bit excited. It was great to see. Tom also watched the way Greg kept glancing at him. Tom had stayed at Greg's until well into the evening and then he'd gone home. He'd been half hoping for an invitation to stay longer, but Greg had hesitated, and Tom hadn't wanted to push. He understood that Greg wanted to be careful, and Tom was realizing that by taking time, he wasn't repeating the mistakes he'd made in the past. Even though just the sight of Greg made his heart beat faster and even now he wanted to take Greg in his arms, kiss him for all he was worth and then slowly strip him down, lay him across the hood of his car, and....

"I'm ready," Davey called, pulling Tom's thoughts back to where they should be.

Tom blinked a few times. "You certainly are," he said, sharing a smile with Greg. He walked over and placed a ball in Davey's hand.

"It's about the size of a softball," Davey said, turning the ball in his hand. Tom activated the ball, and it began to beep.

"In this game, the pitcher and catcher are on your team, and they are sighted. There aren't any strikes. There are six people on a team," Tom explained. "Today we aren't going to play a game or anything. I thought we'd try hitting and running toward the bases, okay?"

"Yeah," Davey said excitedly. "Is Uncle Howard here?"

"Not yet," Greg said, but as he answered a car pulled in, and after a few seconds, Howard got out of the car and then Token jumped out, taking his place at Howard's side. Sophia got out of the backseat, and Gordy came around and guided Howard to where they waited.

"Tom was just explaining things," Davey said as they approached. He held out the ball, and Tom took it, then placed it in Howard's hands.

Tom went over what they would be doing. "Greg is going to pitch, and he'll say 'ready' and then 'pitch' as he releases the ball. He wants you to hit it, because he's on your team, so he'll be gentle and do his best to place the ball in the right position. I'm going to catch. If you get a hit, the bases will activate and buzz." Tom guided Davey to the home base and let him feel it. Gordy did the same for Howard. Then he activated the other base, and Davey ran toward it. When he reached the base, he held on to it, grinning back at them. Tom activated the other base, and Davey ran toward that one. Greg caught him and whirled Davey around.

Howard was more reticent, and they spent a while activating the bases and letting Davey and Howard run between them so they could get the feel for the ground. "Normally we'd play on a flat field instead of a diamond. I'm close to permission to use the soccer field at the high school. The game only has three bases, so it doesn't fit a regular baseball diamond, but I'll work that out. For now, let's have some fun."

"Can I bat?" Davey asked, ready to jump out of his skin.

"Sure," Tom said. He went to get a bat while Greg helped Davey into a helmet, and then Tom got him into position while Greg took one of the balls. "You're supposed to be twenty feet away," Tom told him. Greg got into position, and Tom put on a glove and got into position behind Davey. "Home plate is right in front of you. Remember that your dad is on your team, so no one is trying to fool you."

"Go, Davey!" Sophia cried from where she sat with Token on the bottom row of the bleachers.

"Ready," Greg said and drew back his arm. "Pitch." He threw the ball, and it beeped as it got closer.

Davey swung and missed.

Tom caught the ball and threw it back. "That was your dad's fault," he said and helped Davey get back on place. "Keep your ear on the ball. It may take a few attempts, but don't worry about it." Tom got back into position.

"You can do it, Davey!" Sophia yelled.

"Ready.... pitch," Greg said.

Davey swung and missed.

"Listen for it," Tom said. "You're used to seeing the ball, and that's what you're trying to do. So use the sound to visualize it." He took the bat from Davey's hands, getting another idea. "Maybe we're moving too fast. Your dad and I are going to throw the ball back and forth." He motioned for Gordy to bring Howard closer. "Just listen to the ball as we throw it. You can follow it by the sound and learn to recognize it as it approaches."

Davey began to fidget.

"You learned to hit before you lost your sight, didn't you?" Howard asked Davey.

"Yeah," he answered.

"Then be patient. You'll be slugging that ball before you know it," Howard said, placing his hands on Davey's shoulders.

"Say 'ready, pitch' just like you did when you were throwing to Davey," Tom said, and Greg nodded.

He threw, and Tom caught it. Back and forth the ball went, with Greg saying, "Ready... pitch," over and over again.

"Do you hear it, Davey?" Howard asked. "You can tell when it's getting close."

"I can almost see it coming," Davey said.

"Good." Tom stood up and threw the ball to Greg. "Try to bat again, and this time use all your senses to try to make contact."

Howard moved away with Gordy's help, and Tom got Davey in place.

"Ready... pitch," Greg said and threw the ball.

Davey swung and missed. Tom caught it and threw it back.

"Try again, only swing to the sound of the ball rather than what your dad says. Use the sound the ball makes and then hit it." Tom got into position, and Greg threw the ball. Davey swung and connected, sending the ball past the base and rolling into the outfield.

"I did it," Davey whooped and then dropped the bat and ran for the buzzing base. He reached it with another whoop. Tom activated the other base, and Davey ran over to it, yelling as reached it, "Dad, I hit the ball."

"You certainly did," Greg said.

"You try, Uncle Howard," Davey said.

Howard agreed, and Gordy helped him stand in the batter's box. Then he showed Howard how to hold the bat and swing. They pitched a few balls, and Howard eventually connected, sending the ball rolling along the third base line. Sophia yelled for Howard to run, and he ran to the base and then walked to the other base when Tom activated it.

"I think this is for the young," Howard said. "Token and I will be the mascots."

They got Davey into position, and Greg pitched some more balls. Some were strikes, but Davey got in some solid hits. The skills he'd had from Little League were transferring slowly to the new game.

"What's this?" a man asked, walking over from the other field, holding out his hand as he approached Tom. "Peter Crawford. I'm the coach of the Tigers."

"Tom Spangler," Tom said, shaking hands. "It's beep baseball," he said.

"It looks… different," he said. "I've been watching you and can't quite figure it out."

Greg came in from the pitching area and guided Davey over. Tom saw Peter's eyes widen when the realization dawned on him.

"He's blind." His mouth hung open, and he looked at the bases.

Tom placed a ball in his hand. "Everything is designed to make noise. There are a number of differences from traditional baseball, but the idea is largely the same. We just got the equipment and we were working with Davey here. He played Little League until his sight faded."

"It looks rather easy," Peter said.

"That's because you can see the ball. Hitters and fielders are blind. Catchers and pitchers are sighted. I dare say it isn't as easy as it looks."

"Are you trying to start a league?"

"I think that would be cool, but mostly I'm hoping to get some other kids involved so they can have fun," Tom explained.

"The equipment must be expensive," Peter commented.

Tom smiled. "Money isn't an issue, not for this. It's about allowing kids to play who wouldn't get the opportunity otherwise. Some of the blind support organizations in the area are publicizing what we're doing." Tom pulled out his wallet and extracted one of his cards.

"I'll let the league know. Maybe they can help." Peter took the card and put it in his pocket. Tom shook his hand again and then turned back to the group.

"Are you up for more?" Tom asked. Davey obviously was. "Then let's field. When the ball is hit, the runner is out if the fielders pick up the ball before they reach the base. So your dad will take you into the field, and I'll hit the ball in your direction. All you need to do is pick it up. Can you do that?" Tom asked.

"I'll try," Davey said.

Greg led him out onto the field, and Tom hit the ball. It rolled toward and past him. Davey raced after it and managed to find it. He held it up in triumph.

"I could really follow it," he said.

Greg took the ball and threw it back. Tom hit another one, and Davey took off. He reached the ball more quickly this time.

"He's fearless," Gordy said from behind him.

"I think he's home," Tom said, as Greg threw him the ball.

He hit it again. It bounced right past Davey as he scrambled to stop it. Tom watched Davey turn and then fall to the ground. He saw Greg rush over, but Davey was already up and going for the ball. He reached it and held it high. "This is one of the things he's been missing. He played baseball before, and now he can again." Tom hit another one, and Davey raced for it. This time he came up with the ball before it got by him.

"You're making it easy for him," Gordy said.

"Of course. He needs the confidence to run and reach, and a little success is a great motivator," Tom said, looking at Howard. "He can play too, if he wants."

"Howard has never seen baseball or any sport. I doubt he feels the need, but we'll both be here to do anything we can," Gordy explained.

Tom caught the ball Greg threw and hit it one more time, this one a little harder. It whizzed by Davey, and he ran to get it.

"He's very good." Greg looked proud.

Tom nodded his agreement. "Let's call it a day," he called.

Greg guided Davey in, and they gathered up all the equipment. Sophia ran up to Davey, ponytail flying.

"You did great," she said and then turned to Tom. "Do you think I could play too?"

That had never occurred to him. "I don't see why not. We'd need to get you a blindfold, but that could work." He turned to Gordy and Howard. "Talk it over with your uncles, but it would be nice to have another player. We need six for a team."

"I will," Sophia said and hurried over to Davey. The two of them chattered while the men packed the equipment up and carried it to Tom's trunk.

"Are there additional things we need?" Greg asked as he brought the last of the equipment.

"I have four other balls as well as chargers. For fielding, I was wondering about gloves, but it would probably be better if they used their hands. Maybe with thin gloves for protection."

"What if we don't get any more players?" Greg asked.

"We'll figure that out," Tom said. "For now it doesn't matter, and if necessary I'll order a bunch of blindfolds and we'll see if other kids are willing to join in, sighted or not." He closed the trunk. "Why don't you and Davey come over to the house? We can have some lunch, and Davey can explore a new place."

"That would be nice," Greg agreed. "I'll get Davey in the car, and we'll follow you."

Tom invited Howard, Gordy, and Sophia as well, but they had another commitment, so Tom waited for Davey and Greg and then got in his car and drove the short distance home, making sure Greg stayed behind him.

"This is your place?" Greg asked once they'd parked and gotten out of the car. "I've driven by here a number of times and always wondered what it looked like inside." Greg turned to Davey. "Do you remember the house with lots of colors and the round tower? That's Tom's house."

"Cool. Does it have round rooms?" Davey asked.

"Yes. Come on inside and you can explore it," Tom said, extremely pleased. He took Davey's arm, and Greg allowed him to guide Davey.

Once inside, Tom described the house to Davey so he could find his way around. But what made him happiest were the sounds of awe he heard from Greg. "This is amazing. How did you get your hands on this place? There must have been a line of people wanting to get it."

"It didn't look like this when I bought it. I had to have the woodwork touched up, carpet removed, wallpaper stripped, and in some places, paint removed. They had done some awful things to the poor house. In the office"—he gestured toward the room in the front—"they actually paneled the walls with cheap crap. I had it removed and then had the plaster repaired. Crown moldings had to be fabricated and replaced. And the bathroom upstairs—it was two rooms, so I had them combined."

"You must have had workmen here for months," Greg said.

"There were a lot of people. The kitchen had to be done too, so I had a dozen people working here at one point. But I wanted it done, so the bath people worked upstairs, the kitchen people downstairs, and others in between."

Davey had made his way to the staircase and started feeling his way up the banister.

"Be careful," Greg said, and Davey retraced his steps back to Greg. "Are the windows original?"

"Yeah. They were here, but in terrible shape."

"Did you have them sent out for repair?"

"No. That I did myself. I turned the basement into a glass studio. I've done that kind of work since I was a teenager. I wanted to be the next Tiffany, but it's just a hobby. I'm working on one of the windows from the dining room now. It's the last one I have to do."

Tom led the way to the office. "I wish I had something for you to do. I have the stereo in here, and it's hooked to the computer."

"That's all right. I brought my tablet," Davey said. "Dad loaded some cool voice software so I can control it better."

Tom led Davey to the most comfortable chair in the house. Davey sat and immediately settled and began issuing commands to the tablet. He pulled some earbuds out of his pocket and put them in.

"He's listening to *Harry Potter* now. You really opened things up with the audiobooks thing," Greg said.

"That's good. I'll show you the rest of the house if you like," Tom offered.

Greg told Davey where he was going to be, and then Tom led Greg from room to room. "The fireplace mantel had been painted, and we found that chestnut under eight layers of paint. It took a lot of work to get that crap off, but it was worth it. The pocket doors still need to be stripped, but I could only take so much upheaval at once. I'll have those done eventually." Tom led Greg through the original butler's pantry to the kitchen.

"While I've tried to restore as much of the house as I can to its original splendor, I believe in modern kitchens and bathrooms," Tom explained as they stepped into the room. "There was nothing original in this room at all. As far as I can tell, it had been gutted in the fifties, so I used natural wood and materials to make a space that felt comfortable and not fussy."

"I love the granite," Greg said, and Tom watched him run his hand over it. He stepped closer and wrapped Greg in his arms.

"I've wanted to do this all morning," Tom said, and then he kissed him hard. "Every time I looked at you, I thought about kissing your sweet mouth." Greg chuckled once Tom broke the kiss. "That wasn't the reaction I was hoping for."

"It isn't you. It's just that no one has ever said things like that to me. It sounded sort of… strange."

"Okay," Tom said. "How about this? When we're together, I have a hard time taking my eyes off you. We were playing the game and my attention kept wandering to the pitcher instead of staying on the ball." His instinct at the moment was to be aggressive and go for what he wanted. It was what he was used to doing. But that wasn't what Greg needed, so he backed away slightly. "I have this feeling that sometimes I scare you."

"Not scare, but I wonder what you want," Greg said.

"I don't want anything other than some of your time and attention." Tom motioned. "Look around. I have plenty. The garage has cars in it that cost more than most people make in years. I can buy whatever I want. But I want what I can't buy." Tom leaned back against the kitchen island. "This is so hard to explain. I don't tell people what I have and where I live because I don't want them to like me for my money. And yet in the past I've always used my money to get what I want, including the interest of other people. Like, I'd meet a guy in a club, and we'd go out on a few dates. Then I'd decide to impress him, so I'd show up for our next date in a Ferrari. He'd be impressed, and I'd have his attention, which is what I wanted. But I'd screwed up the relationship." Tom began to fidget. "I almost made that same mistake the other day, but…."

"What is it you want, Tom?" Greg asked. "Why would you want me? I'm not that interesting, and I come with baggage." He cringed when he said the word. "You know what I mean."

"You have a kind heart," Tom said. "And it's been a long time since I've met someone like that." He placed his hand on Greg's chest. "What I want is the same thing most people want—for someone to care about me for me." Tom stroked Greg's cheek and then his hair. "I know you have a lot going on in your life. All I'm asking is that you let me be part of it."

"Why would you want to be part of it? My life is a mess. The minute I drop Davey off at school, I go to work and get as much done as I can so I can be there when Davey comes home. He takes almost all my remaining energy, and once I get him in bed, I go back to work. In between there's all the household chores and… life."

"What are you saying?" Tom asked a little fearfully.

"I don't know what I'm saying other than my life is so busy right now that I don't have the time or the energy for much outside of Davey, work, and keeping myself together."

Tom opened his mouth to say he could help, but stopped. He was about to make another of his mistakes. "How about we take things a day at a time? We spent yesterday at the beach and today we played at the park. Both were fun."

Greg sighed. "Yes. But neither was a date or any time alone. It was with Davey and other friends. I can't see us getting a lot of time alone. There are too many demands on my time." Greg closed his eyes, and Tom highly suspected that Greg was becoming overwhelmed.

A phone chirped, and Tom pulled his cell out of his pocket. Greg did the same and groaned loudly.

"What is it?" Tom asked.

"Davey's mother is coming to town to see him," Greg said.

"That's good. Maybe she wants to be part of his life, and you can work things out with her," Tom suggested.

Greg shook his head definitively. "No. I don't know why she's coming, but if the conversation I had yesterday is any indication, this visit isn't going to be pretty." The phone beeped again. "She's asking where she can stay."

"Tell her the Hampton Inn," Tom answered. "I know what you're thinking, but you don't have to put up your ex-wife in your house. If things go as badly as you suspect, then you'd have no way out. Best to keep her at a distance for both you and Davey."

Greg bit his lower lip and then typed on his phone and sent the message. When his phone beeped again, Greg read the message and then turned the phone to him. Tom read what she had sent and said, "All the more reason. She has definite anger-management issues. And don't delete those texts—you might need them."

"Should I answer her?"

"I wouldn't. Let her stew and she'll get the idea. If she calls, let it go to voice mail."

"She is Davey's mother."

"Who hasn't been part of his life in years," Tom countered. "You don't owe her anything. If you want to respond, ask her when she'll be here and tell her she needs to call before she comes over. You and Davey have appointments and a schedule that can't be changed."

Greg began to answer and paused. "Do you always do that?"

"Do what?"

"Take charge like that?" Greg clarified. "Not that your idea isn't good."

"It's one of my many faults. I always think I have the answer to everyone else's problems, but I rarely see the answers to my own with as much clarity," Tom said, as Greg sent the text.

"I added that we can have dinner when she arrives. I want to sound firm without being mean," Greg said. "Even if she can be abrasive, she is coming to see Davey, and he should know his mother other than the occasional phone call."

Tom nodded. "See? You have a good heart."

The text Greg received in response was much more civil, explaining when she'd be arriving and asking when she would be able to see Davey. Greg answered it and then put the phone back into his pocket.

"Like I was saying, you were nice to her even when she was rude and pushy. I would be equally rude and pushy back, but you were kind." Tom smiled.

"Dad," Davey called.

Tom backed away, and they walked toward his voice.

Davey stood in the hall. "I'm sorry." He turned back the way he'd come, and Greg saw the tablet on the floor. "I heard it break. It slipped off my lap and I didn't catch it in time."

Tom walked into the office. The glass was cracked in multiple places. It would work, but was clearly unusable. "It's all right. We'll get another one. Maybe Uncle Howard can suggest what we can get." Greg put his arms around Davey to soothe him.

"I have one he can use," Tom offered. "Howard installed some of the voice command and recognition software on it a few months ago for testing purposes. It's a few years older than the one you had, but it should get you through until you can get another." Tom pulled open his desk drawer and found the tablet along with the charger. He plugged it in near Davey's chair, figuring the battery was probably either very low or dead. Then Tom turned it on and waited for it to boot up. "You'll need to be careful of the cord," Tom explained, guiding Davey's hand so he knew where it was. Tom then turned on the screen-reading and voice-command features.

"Does the voice have a name? Like Siri for iPhones," Davey asked.

"Ralph," Tom answered. "Your Uncle Howard has a real sense of humor. Just follow the instructions. Ralph will guide you." Tom left the room and Greg followed him into the living room.

"You don't have to let him use your tablet. Look what he did with the other one."

"It's older, and he's not going to hurt it." Damage was the last thing on his mind. "Things are going to break. Ask Howard. He'll tell you about things he's broken. It goes with the territory, and unless you cleanse his environment of everything, it'll happen. I wouldn't keep a Ming vase around Davey, but...." Tom chuckled. "He's ten. He'd break things whether he could see or not. I did. Take his tablet home. It's still working. You can probably get the data off it and then transfer it to the next one."

"How can you be so patient?" Greg asked.

Tom motioned toward the sofa, and Greg sat down. "He's a great kid, and the truth is I always wanted to have a child, but never had the chance to start a family. I thought about it more than once, but I wasn't going to do it alone. Raising kids properly is hard enough. My folks wouldn't agree with that, but they had people who lightened the load and put distance between us. I don't want to do that."

"So you hope to have a baby someday?" Greg asked with a smile. "I've met a few guys who found out I had a kid and ran for the hills."

"Yeah, I can imagine that." Tom thought of Skip in New York, who would rather die than get near a child of any type. "I'd like a child of my own if things are right. If they're not, I can live with that too. Sometimes life throws you curveballs. It did for Howard when he got Sophia. I know he doesn't regret it for a second, and I wouldn't either, but he told me it was a difficult decision for him. Not that he didn't want Sophia—he did. But it was hard for him to decide because of what he thought was best for her."

"Because he was blind," Greg finished. "He told me about that once."

"So then you know you have nothing to worry about with Davey. He will be just as capable as Howard and just as able to have a full, rich life where he'll be loved and cared for the way Howard is."

"How did we get back to that?" Greg asked.

"I'm wily and I'm trying to make a point. You deserve that same thing." Tom shifted from his chair to the seat next to Greg. "Davey can't be allowed to let his blindness dictate everything in his life, and you can't allow it to dictate everything in yours."

"Okay," Greg said. "You made your point."

"Good. Now I get to emphasize it," Tom retorted and kissed him. Now was not the time to take things further, but Tom made sure Greg understood that he was willing—more than willing, *aching*—to do just that. But he couldn't. Tom stifled a groan and leaned against Greg. Davey came out of the office, feeling his way. "Take six steps and you'll be across the hall. Just follow my voice and you'll enter the living room." Tom kept talking until Davey approached the sofa. Then he directed him to the chair. "You're doing really well. Are you hungry? I can get something to eat and drink." He should have thought of that earlier. Having Greg close had scrambled his brain. He got up and hurried to the kitchen.

There was snack food in the refrigerator, but he wished he'd planned ahead better. He found some small tacos in the freezer, placed some on a cookie sheet, and put them in the oven. Then he got some plates and drinks together before starting to carrying things into the dining room. He figured it would be easier to sit and eat at the table.

"She'll be here on Tuesday," he heard Greg say to Davey.

"Why is she coming? Is it because I can't see?" Davey asked.

"I think so," Greg said.

"Then she can stay away. I don't want her to come." He folded his arms over his chest.

"Davey," Greg said quietly. "She's coming all this way."

"Over two years, Dad. She hasn't seen me in over two years," he said dramatically. "Now she's only coming because I'm blind. Well, she can leave me alone for all I care. I don't want her here and I'm not going anywhere with her."

"We don't talk that way," Greg scolded, but Tom caught his expression and saw that Greg was doing his best to keep from laughing. "And I'm not any happier than you are, but we need to be nice. She is your mother. I expect she won't stay long, and then things will get back to normal. I did tell her that we aren't changing our routine, so you'll still go to therapy and your classes for the blind." Greg smiled at him.

Tom nodded as he finished unloading the tray and went back into the kitchen. He waited until the tacos were done, then transferred them to a plate and brought the last of a light lunch to the dining room.

Greg brought Davey to the table and spent a few minutes making up his plate and explaining where everything was. Then they all began to eat.

"I don't know why she has to come," Davey said.

"You don't want to spend time with your mother?" Tom asked.

"Why? The last time all she did was tell me what to do and act bossy. She didn't want to do anything fun and then she left, no phone call or nothing. She lives in Florida, less than a couple hours from Disney World, but does she invite me down? No. I asked and she said she was too busy. So I'm too busy for her."

"Wow," Tom mouthed, and Greg rolled his eyes.

"Joyce has been very driven since the divorce," Greg explained.

Tom wondered why he was making excuses for her. Greg was probably trying to be nice, but it still made Tom curious. He was becoming more and more interested in meeting this woman. She couldn't be all bad; she'd given birth to Davey. But Greg had been the one to raise him, so maybe she didn't deserve any credit after all.

"Eat your lunch and worry about your mother later."

Davey scowled but slowly began to eat. He was indeed much neater than he'd been the first time Tom had come to dinner. "I don't like her."

"Okay. You don't have to like her," Greg agreed.

They ate in near silence for a while.

"When can we play beep ball again?" Davey asked. "Do you think you can get more players?"

"How about Wednesday evening after your dad gets home from work?" Tom suggested, speaking to Davey, but looking at Greg, who nodded. "As long as the weather is nice. I'll see if Uncle Howard and Uncle Gordy can bring Sophia so she can play too." That seemed to make Davey forget the business about his mother, at least for a while, and he talked about the game through the rest of lunch.

In the midafternoon, Greg and Davey got ready to leave. Tom said good-bye to Davey, who hugged him and thanked him for letting him play beep ball.

"Call me, okay?" Tom asked, and Greg nodded.

"Maybe next Friday. I can see if Gordy or Ken will watch Davey," Greg said excitedly. "Hopefully Joyce won't stay too long and things can get back to normal."

Tom pulled Greg into a hug, holding him tightly. "Don't let her get to you. I'll be here if you need me or just want to talk, and if nothing else, I'll meet you at the park at seven on Wednesday." He kissed Greg and then let him go. "I'll talk to you soon."

Greg guided Davey toward the door. "Thank you for letting me use the tablet," Davey said as they left the house.

"No problem," Tom called. He waved to Greg and watched as he and Davey got into the car and then drove off. Tom closed the door and wandered through the living and dining rooms, taking care of the dishes and carrying them to the kitchen. He loaded the dishwasher and got it running, then turned out the lights and wandered through the house. He loved the place, but up till now, he hadn't realized how large the house was, or how empty. Having Greg and Davey there had filled the house with life for a few hours, but now it just seemed big and quiet.

Needing someone to talk with, Tom decided to catch up on all the New York gossip and picked up his phone. He looked up Skip in his contacts and pressed send. It was well after noon, so he should be up. Tom smiled when his call was answered, and grinned when Skip squealed in delight on hearing his voice.

He loved his life here and had no real interest in going back to New York, but sometimes hearing about the familiar calmed him, and after two years of invitations, he finally convinced Skip to come for a visit. Tom wasn't sure what Skip would think of this town "in the middle of nowhere," as Skip put it.

"So do I get to meet this boyfriend with a kid?" Skip asked with a giggle. "I can't believe you're dating a guy who has a ten-year-old."

"What's so hard to believe?" Tom asked. "I've always liked kids."

"Club kids, but not kid kids so much," Skip countered.

"I'm not the same as I was then," Tom explained. "Things aren't the same here. It's hard for me to describe, but I feel like a grown-up here. Living in New York was like living at Disneyland. Here I feel like an adult and I can make a difference. New York is huge, and everything happens so fast and happens to you. Here, I get to make a difference. You'll see when you come."

"Yeah, okay, I will, but I still can't see you dating a guy with a kid. A blind kid, no less."

"Skip," Tom said warningly.

"I'm not being rude. I'm just surprised, that's all. This must be some kid," Skip said.

"Think about it: he and his dad found out he was losing his sight about three months ago, and then a few weeks ago, he went nearly blind. Now Davey says he rarely sees anything at all. All this within a short period of time. And he's adjusting and learning how to cope and adapt. He's startlingly amazing, and so is his dad. Greg guides Davey without trying to overpower him. He's a wonderful dad and has an incredible heart."

"Aw, crap," Skip said. "You're falling in love with the guy, aren't you? Don't answer, because you'll want to say you aren't, and I can hear the truth in your voice. At least tell me he's good in bed."

Tom didn't answer right away.

"Shit," Skip went on. "Is he that bad?"

"Skip, we haven't...." Tom began, and he heard complete silence on the other end of the line.

"Double crap. You're falling for a guy you haven't even had sex with?" The phone clinked, and Tom looked at the display, thinking they'd been disconnected, but the call still showed as active. "I'm pulling up flights right now."

"This isn't the end of the world," Tom said, but he knew it was useless. Once Skip got his drama up, there was no stopping him. "We're exploring things."

"Please. One of my best friends is falling head over heels for a guy, and he hasn't even found out if he's good in bed. What if he isn't? You'll start saying things like it isn't that important or it's how we feel about each other, or some other rot like that."

"Skip, this isn't necessary."

"Oh, yes it is," Skip said. "Yes, there's a flight on Tuesday morning. I have to change planes in Detroit. Yuck, I hate that airport! But I'll be there before noon. Do I need a car, or can I use one of yours? I'll text you the details in a few minutes. Is there anything you want me to bring? I'll stop at Zabar's and pick up some provisions. There we are—I'm all set. I get in at eleven Tuesday morning." Skip finally stopped talking.

"Are you winded? That was quite a stretch, even for you." Tom grinned. Skip always figured if the other person couldn't get a word in, then they couldn't argue and he would get his way. Tom had always figured Skip could talk his way to Middle East peace. Both sides would give up and give him what he wanted simply to get him to stop talking. "What if I had plans?"

Skip scoffed. "You would have told me already. Come on, Tom, I know you, and it's been too long." He paused. "I'm looking forward to seeing you. Okay?"

"You're impossible," Tom teased. "I'm looking forward to seeing you too." Tom hung up the phone, feeling better and wondering what the hell he'd just let himself in for. It was going to be a very interesting week. He hoped all the plans didn't blow up in his face.

TUESDAY MORNING, near eleven, Tom drove to the airport and parked in the lot. He walked into the small terminal and looked at the board. Six flights were displayed, and Skip's puddle jumper from Detroit showed as on time. Someone had had the forethought to put rocking chairs in the waiting area, and Tom settled in one, watching the arrival area. It wasn't long before he heard Skip's animated voice echoing through the terminal. Then he saw him, striding next to a tall woman. The two were talking back and forth as another man followed quietly, glancing at them every few seconds and then returning his attention to his phone. Skip said good-bye and broke away, rushed over, hugged him tight, and then kissed him on the cheek.

"I made it in one piece. They had us on this dinky plane. It was so small there wasn't even first class." Tom expected Skip to laugh, but he was serious. "I did meet an interesting woman. She's here from Florida to visit her son, and since there was nothing else to do, she and I talked for most of the flight. She's traveling with some doctor. I offered to switch seats, but it didn't seem to matter. He spent his time either with his head buried in his laptop or shuffling through papers. I asked if he was her husband, but she shook her head and winked at me." Skip giggled. "A doctor who makes house calls, or maybe booty calls."

They walked to the baggage claim.

"I'm glad you had a good trip," Tom said.

"It wasn't bad. The flights were on time, and I stopped for a drink in Detroit, which made things bearable," Skip said. "The airport's a little small."

"So is the town, Skip," Tom said. "There's a university, but mostly this is a small town." The belt started moving, and bags began to appear. It was easy to spot Skip's. His set of Louis Vuitton luggage stood out like a sore thumb. "How long are you planning to stay?" Tom asked as he hauled the second bag off the belt.

"Just a few days, but I brought goodies that filled this bag, and I didn't know what we would be doing, so I brought clothes for every occasion."

"Have a nice stay," the women told Skip as she passed.

"You too, Joyce," Skip said. Tom nearly dropped the bag he was carrying. "What?"

Tom swallowed hard. "Let's get to the car." He led the way out of the terminal to where he'd parked the car. After putting the bags in the trunk, they got inside. Tom started the engine and cranked the AC to start cooling the interior. "Okay, tell me what you and that woman talked about. Did she say why she was here and what the doctor was for?"

"She said she was here to visit her kid and that she'd convinced her doctor friend to come along. He said what kind of doctor he was, but I can't remember the word. Not that it mattered; he was a dead fish, but she was interesting. Why? What's going on?"

"I'm not sure, but I believe she's Greg's ex-wife and the son she's coming to visit is Davey. I have a bad feeling about this."

"If she's the kid's mother...," Skip said.

"If what Greg says is true, then she makes my mother look like a saint and yours mother of the year. At least ours were around. Greg was able to prove during the divorce that she only wanted Davey for the child support, and other than a few cards and gifts, her only son hasn't seen her in years. Now she shows up with a doctor in tow. She's up to something."

"Okay." Skip settled back in the seat. "What are you going to do?"

Tom put the car in reverse and backed out of the parking space. "We're going to get your stuff to the house, and then I'm going to call Greg and let him know what's going on."

"Why not do it now?"

"Because I need a chance to think, and the short drive home will give me that," Tom said, exiting the airport and then driving as fast as he dared the few miles to his house in town.

"Nice place," Skip said when Tom pulled into the drive and then up to the garage, parking outside the last door. Tom popped the trunk and then handed Skip the keys. "You can drive this while you're in town."

They carried the bags inside, and Tom called Greg, but the call went to voice mail. While Skip got himself settled, Tom paced in the living room and then tried again. It went to voice mail once again. "Greg, it's Tom. Please call me."

"Did you get him?" Skip asked, descending the stairs. Tom shook his head. "This place is amazing. You described it to me, but I had no idea. You could turn this into a bed-and-breakfast."

Tom smiled. "Perfect. I'll hire you to clean the bathrooms and make the beds. I'll even get you a maid's uniform."

"There's no need to be mean," Skip said. "I just meant this house is bed-and-breakfast quality."

"Thanks," Tom said, picking up his phone and trying again. No answer. He hung up when the message came on. "Let's go," he said. "We're going to drive over there and see what's happening."

Tom locked the front door and led the way through the house and out the kitchen door. They walked the short distance to the garage. "Go ahead and pull the BMW inside," Tom said, raising the door. He lifted another door and walked to the red Ferrari. He opened the door and slid into the driver's seat. Once Skip had pulled the car inside the garage and closed the door, he got in the passenger seat of the Ferrari and buckled up.

The engine came to life with a roar, and Tom backed out of the drive and pressed the button to lower the garage door. Then he backed down the drive and onto the street, flipped the car into gear and took off toward Greg's.

"You could let me drive this or the Lamborghini instead of the Beemer," Skip said.

Tom simply scowled and accelerated.

A few minutes later they rolled to a stop in Greg's driveway. Tom turned off the engine and got out, then strode up to the front door. He wasn't sure if anyone was home, so he went ahead and rang the bell. The door opened and Greg blinked at him. "Tom, I wasn't expecting you."

"I tried calling but I just got voice mail," he said.

"I must have left my phone in the bedroom while I was getting things ready for Joyce. Come on in," Greg said, pushing open the door.

"This is my friend Skip, from New York. This is Greg. Is Davey in class?" Tom asked, and Greg nodded.

"It's good to meet you," Greg said to Skip as they shook hands.

Tom got right to the point. "Skip just arrived, and I believe he shared the flight with Joyce. The thing is, she was traveling with a doctor. Since I couldn't get you on the phone, I figured I'd try stopping over to let you know. I don't know what she's up to."

"Thanks. Excuse me a minute." Greg left the room and returned a minute later with his phone.

"We didn't want to disturb you, but I was concerned," Tom admitted, moving a little closer. He leaned in and gave Greg a soft kiss on the lips.

"It's all right. Are we still on for tomorrow? Davey has been talking about beep ball for days. I swear he's been to every website he can find to try to learn more."

"Of course."

"Ken and Patrick are going to watch Davey next Saturday night. He, Hanna, and Sophia have planned a sleepover, so I was thinking...."

Tom pulled Greg into his arms and kissed him again, this time deeper and with a lot more energy.

"I take it you approve."

"Uh-huh," Tom murmured. "I'm going to show Skip around, but if something happens and you need backup, just call. I can be back here in a few minutes if you need me."

"Thanks. I'm sure I'll be fine, but I appreciate the offer." Greg returned his kiss, and Tom turned to leave. "I'll see you tomorrow at the park. Howard said the Lions Club in town found a few other kids who were interested in playing, so they've passed on the invitation."

"Excellent, I'll see you then," Tom said. "And I was serious before."

"I promise if I need any help, I'll call," Greg said with a small smile.

Tom and Skip left the house and walked to the car, then slid into the leather seats.

"You did the right thing," Skip said. "You can't force him to allow you to help." Skip shifted in the low-slung seat. "He has his pride, and you wouldn't be interested in him if he didn't have a certain amount of inner strength, so don't worry."

Tom nodded and started the engine, then backed out of the drive, wishing he felt better about this.

CHAPTER
Seven

GREG WATCHED Tom and his friend leave then closed the door. He smiled, pleased at the concern and care Tom had shown for him and for Davey. He'd rushed over to tell him what he'd found out. That had been very thoughtful and told Greg quite a bit. He'd been reluctant and standoffish as far as Tom had been concerned, he knew that, but now he was thinking he might have been wrong. Maybe, he allowed himself to think, maybe Tom's feelings were real. He had to be sure, not only for his sake, but for Davey's. Greg knew he was developing feelings for Tom, but he refused to name them. To do so would give them power, and he wasn't ready for that. He was willing to do as Tom had said the last time they were together and take things one day at a time. He could do that. But was it fair to Davey? Greg walked back to his office. He had plenty of work to do. He sat down and stared at the design on his computer screen.

It all seemed distant and strange. He couldn't concentrate on what was there, his mind returning to Tom. Davey adored him, and Greg was pleased, but that adoration could come at a cost if things didn't work out with him and Tom. Not only could Greg get hurt, but Davey could, as well, and Greg couldn't have that. Davey had already been hurt enough.

Greg checked the time. He had to pick up Davey in an hour, so he gave up on work and decided he might as well get some things done around the house. So he dusted and vacuumed for a while, but ended up putting everything away and staring at the space around him. He'd often wondered if he should put things away because of Davey— remove things he might break or damage. He thought about doing that now, but didn't. This was their home, and whether Davey could see them or not, he wanted him surrounded by pictures and memories of the things they'd done together. So what if Davey couldn't see them—they were part of their home, and Davey would know they were there. More importantly, Davey would know if they were gone. Greg wasn't sure when it had started, but Davey was becoming as perceptive as Howard. Greg lowered himself onto the sofa and enjoyed the quiet for a little while.

When it was time, he got up and left the house to pick up Davey at school. Sometimes the classes included him, but right now the teachers wanted to work with just Davey. He'd almost reached the car when his phone rang. Without looking, he knew it was Joyce.

"Hello," Greg said quietly.

"I got into town and I was wondering when I could come over and see Davey," Joyce began without preamble.

"I'm going to pick up Davey from classes now. We should be back in about half an hour, so you can come by the house then," he said levelly, deciding to keep all the questions to himself for now. He figured they'd be answered in time. "We don't have plans for dinner, so if you'd like to join us, I had planned to take Davey to one of the local diners." He was going to be hospitable, but he didn't want her spending any more time than necessary under his roof.

"I thought I'd take him to dinner," Joyce said, pushy as ever.

"Like I said, you are welcome to join us for dinner," Greg repeated. "Anyway, I need to pick Davey up. You can stop by in half an hour if you like."

"All right," she agreed, and Greg hung up. Then he got in the car and drove to a small brick building. The school was staffed mostly by volunteers and used classroom space donated by the local school district. He got out and walked inside, going to the office. They knew who he was, and Davey joined him a few minutes later.

"How was class?"

"Good," he said. "I'm learning a lot about listening."

"We're starting classes in Braille in the fall, and we think Davey is going to do fine," Davey's instructor, Christine, said. "He's doing very well, and we believe he should be able to attend some regular classes when school starts. He'll need special attention and support, but that can be provided. And once he learns Braille, he can be set up with the same textbooks as the other students."

"That's excellent," Greg said. "I knew you'd do well," he said to Davey.

"We have some exercises you can do with him at home to help strengthen his skills," Christine said, handing Greg a sheet of paper. "He told us he's going to play beep ball?" The instructor sounded skeptical.

"Beep baseball is designed for blind players. We're just starting. You'd be welcome to come watch if you like. We're meeting at Grafton Park tomorrow at seven. Mostly what we do is practice and have fun. But we'd like to develop a team."

She still didn't look convinced.

"Check it out on the Internet. There's even a league. Davey was in Little League," he added, and Christine nodded, her eyes brightening with what Greg took as understanding. "Are you ready to go?" he asked Davey, and he let Davey lead the way out of the building.

"Did Mom get here?" Davey asked once they were in the car.

"Yes. She'll probably be at the house when we get there." Davey had most definitely not warmed to the idea of her visit. "Just be nice. I said she could go to dinner with us at the diner if she wanted."

Davey crossed his arms over his chest and said nothing as they rode home. He didn't have to; his body language screamed that he didn't want to go home. Greg had purposely not mentioned anything to Joyce about Davey's hostility. Let her see what she'd done to Davey and how she'd alienated herself from her son. Maybe Greg should have said something. He'd debated telling her, but in the end he decided to let her see for herself.

"Are we still going to the diner?" Davey still didn't sound happy.

"Yes. I invited your mother to come," Greg repeated, receiving a scowl in return. "Tom stopped by the house earlier today. He has a friend, Skip, in from New York, but I can call and see if they want to come too." This was not going to be pretty, and some support might be in order.

"Okay," Davey said, relaxing slightly. "Is Tom your boyfriend now?"

"I'd like to think so. We haven't talked about it," Greg said. But Tom certainly acted like his boyfriend, and Greg liked that idea. "If he were, would that be okay with you?"

"Yeah. Tom's really nice, and I think he likes you," Davey said. "He talks to you different than when he talks to anyone else. His voice gets lower, and it's like he's only talking to you even when there's a room full of people." Davey quieted

Greg continued driving. He knew Davey had something he was running through his head, but Greg had to let him say it in his own time.

"I want you to be happy, Dad."

They made the turn onto their street, and Greg pulled the car off the road and to a stop. He put it in park and popped off his seat belt. Then he leaned over the seat. "I want you to be happy too. You're the most important person in the world to me."

"I don't want to go anywhere with Mom. I want to stay here with you."

"Of course you're staying here with me. What would make you think you weren't?" Greg asked.

"Well, I've been with you a long time, and I thought it might be Mom's turn now. You also have a boyfriend now, and you need time with him. So I thought you'd send me away with Mom so you could be with Tom." Davey sounded so small, and Greg felt tears well in his eyes.

"Never. You're my son and you're going to stay with me. I'm not sending you off to Florida or anyplace else. This is your home, right here." He hugged Davey tight. "I have a pretty good idea why your mother decided to come for a visit now, and I want you to be nice because she's your mother. But you don't have to do anything you don't want to. She'll probably be waiting for us, if I know Joyce, so we'll talk and find out what she wants. I've said she can go to dinner, and she's welcome, but after that it's up to you. If you don't want to see her anymore, just say so."

"But what if she gets mad at you? The kids in class said she'd blame you for turning me against her," Davey said.

"I can take care of that. Don't worry about what your mother thinks of me. You're old enough to start making some decisions for yourself. So you get to decide what you want and who you spend your time with." Greg hugged Davey one more time. "Now, I'm going to call Tom and ask him to come for dinner, and then we'll go home and face *your mother*." He exaggerated the last words, and Davey giggled.

Greg called Tom, and he and Skip agreed to meet them at the house at five thirty and then go to the Rainbow Rocks Diner. With that done, Greg drove the rest of the way home.

There was a car waiting there, as expected. Greg pulled into the drive and told Davey where they were in relation to the front door. He got out and began walking up the walk using the cane he'd just received to search around him. Greg stayed back and let Davey do it on his own.

"What are you doing?" Joyce said, hurrying up the drive in heels. "He'll fall and get hurt."

Greg turned to her, his gaze shooting daggers. She quieted almost instantly. "He's learning to make his own way," he said softly to her. "You're doing great, Davey. Just a few more feet and then you can turn toward the front door. Don't forget that there's one step." Davey had stopped, but he slowly began moving again. He made the turn and took the single step to the landing, reaching for the front door. When Davey touched the doorknob, he let out a little whoop. Greg released the breath he'd been holding.

"Come on inside," Greg offered and began walking toward the door. "You did great," he told Davey, ruffling his hair before unlocking the door. Davey went inside, and Greg waited. Joyce turned back toward the car she'd come in, and a man got out and strode up the walk to join her. Greg held the door and let the two of them inside.

"Davey, say hello to your mother," he said gently.

Davey moved forward from where he'd been standing, following Greg's voice. When Davey stood next to him, he moved close.

"Davey, it's me," Joyce said. She held out her arms, and Greg rolled his eyes.

"Who is that?" Davey asked, turning toward Greg.

"I'm your mother," Joyce said, visibly shaken.

"Hi, Mom," Davey said without moving away. "Dad said you were coming." He sounded as though he were talking to a stranger, which Joyce mostly was to him.

"Who's this?" Greg asked, indicating the man with Joyce.

She brightened. "This is Dr. Sanjay Patel. He's a noted neurologist from Tampa."

From the way Joyce looked at the doctor, Greg knew instantly that they were sleeping together. Obviously her current marriage was on the rocks and she was trolling for greener pastures.

"He's a friend, and he agreed to come with me to try to help you."

Greg extended his hand, and Sanjay shook it. "It's nice of you to come all this way, but Davey has seen ophthalmologists and neurologists already. His optic nerves have nearly stopped functioning. We're working together to help him learn how to cope and flourish with his blindness." Greg put his arm around Davey's shoulder.

"There are some treatments that could be tried to restimulate the nerves into action. We've had some remarkable successes."

"Are these treatments experimental?" Greg asked as Joyce shot daggers at him that Greg ignored.

"In this country they're considered experimental, yes, but in other parts of the world, they've been used with some success. Joyce asked me to examine her son and determine if he'd be a candidate for the treatment. If he is, she's given her permission for the treatments to be performed," he said levelly, and Joyce looked smug.

"No," Greg said. "Joyce has no authority to give permission for anything as far as Davey is concerned." Greg's anger rose to the surface. "Davey, please go to your room. I need to have a talk with your mother."

"Does it involve me?" he asked defiantly.

Greg leaned down. "Please go, for me? We'll talk later, I promise." This was not the way he'd hoped this visit would start, but he needed to lay down the ground rules for Joyce's visit. He'd honestly hoped that Davey could build some sort of relationship with his mother, but that was not going to work while she was under any delusions. Davey nodded his agreement and slowly made his way down the hall.

Once the bedroom door closed, Greg motioned toward the chairs, to be civil.

"He's my son too, and I want the best I can give him," Joyce said as soon as she sat down.

"Yes, he is your son, but I dispute the second part of your statement," Greg said as evenly as he could. "I don't know why you're here all of a sudden with a doctor in tow, since you haven't been part of Davey's life in years." He paused, trying to figure out how he wanted to handle this.

"That doesn't make her any less Davey's mother," Sanjay said, reaching over to take Joyce's hand.

A low rumble reached his ears, and Greg stood, looking out the front window. Tom's red sports car pulled to a stop right behind Joyce and Sanjay's rental. Sanjay looked as well, and his eyes widened. Greg walked to the door and pulled it open, allowing Tom and Skip to come inside. He made introductions. Davey came out to greet them, giving Tom a huge hug. Tom settled in the chair next to his.

"Davey, would you like to show me your backyard?" Skip asked. Davey looked confused, but after a few seconds, he seemed to get the idea. "Have you ever been to New York?" Skip asked as the two of them made their way toward the back.

"No," Davey answered.

"Well, then, maybe you, Tom, and your dad should come for a visit. We could do some really fun things." Their voices trailed off as they got farther away, but Davey seemed entranced with Skip.

"They'll get along great. They're both at the same maturity level," Tom whispered with a wink.

"What does he have to do with this?" Joyce asked derisively.

"I'm only here for moral support," Tom said, and he took Greg's hand the same way Sanjay still held Joyce's.

"Is Davey going to be okay alone with him?"

"Davey is very self-reliant around the house. Tom and I have worked with him for hours both inside and out so he has markers that he uses as reference points. Everything has been paced. Sure, he still gets frustrated and angry sometimes, but he's coping, and I'm not going to allow anyone to give him false hope." Greg squeezed Tom's hand, glad he was here. "So, as I was saying, since Joyce has provided no support, like the courts ordered, and has not been part of Davey's life for more than two years, I filed suit, and your visitation and custody rights have been terminated."

"What!" Joyce practically screamed. "You did what?"

"Certified letters were sent to your address, notifying you of the action. You never responded, so a summary judgment was entered against you. Basically, it means that your ability to make any sort of decisions as far as Davey is concerned has no validity whatsoever." Greg paused for breath and saw Joyce getting up a head of steam.

"Is that why you came? To assert some sort of authority?" Tom asked. "Greg said you were here to see Davey."

"What is it to you?" Joyce snapped.

Greg knew another insult was just around the corner and opened his mouth to interject.

"I care for Davey and Greg," Tom said.

"You're not part of his family," Joyce retorted.

"Joyce, that's enough," Greg said firmly. "I did what I had to do for Davey's protection. You had no time for him and you were never around. Years of no visits, few phone calls, no help or support, and almost completely ignoring him wasn't endearing to the court or to me. He deserves people in his life who care about him and you obviously don't. You were notified and didn't respond," Greg said.

"You should have called when you found out he was going blind," she said firmly. "I am his mother. You should have called."

Greg took a deep breath to keep his voice under control. There were so many things he wanted to tell her, and they all seemed to want to tumble out at the same time. "Joyce," Greg began, "you said you came here to see Davey and spend some time with him. Instead, you bring a doctor with you and try to take over his medical care. That doesn't make any sense." Greg felt empowered with Tom sitting next to him. Joyce was an in-charge person, and he'd rarely stood up to her in their marriage. But it was easy now. He knew part of that was time and a change in his attitude, but having Tom next to him made it easier. "If you want to spend time with Davey, then go on out there and get to know him."

Joyce shifted uncomfortably. "I want to talk about how we can help Davey get his sight back." She sounded like a broken record.

Tom squeezed his hand, and Greg released the breath he was holding and forced himself to relax. "Do you want to know why we never called you?" Greg asked, and he found he had Joyce's full attention. "We never thought about it. It didn't occur to either of us. You aren't a part of his life in any way." Greg stood up. "I'll be right back." He left the room and went to his own, then returned a few minutes later. "These are the glasses Davey wore a year ago. These are the ones three months after that." He handed each pair to her. "Three months later, he wore these." Then he placed a final pair in her hands. "These were the ones he wore just before he lost his sight. He went through tests and pair after pair of glasses to try to correct his failing vision. During that time you never called, not once. You weren't a part of our lives and haven't been in a long time."

Joyce held the glasses and didn't say a word.

"Look, you have more important things to worry about than what kind of medical care Davey is receiving. When I told him you were coming, he made it clear that he didn't want to see you. He's hurt that you've ignored him all these years. Hell, he's in the backyard with someone he just met because he doesn't want to be in here with you."

"You turned him against me," she accused, and Greg could tell she was seconds from tears.

"I did no such thing. You did that on your own," Greg said and he felt Tom shift a little closer. It was nice knowing he was supported. "I might not be the perfect father, but I'm here and I try. As far as Davey is concerned, you have quite a mountain to climb to be a part of his life. He feels like you abandoned him, and now, because he can't see and you feel sorry for him, you want to show up and be part of his life. Well, Joyce, he isn't buying it, and neither am I. I've never been heavy-handed, you know that, but if I think you're going to hurt him in any way, I will make sure you are not part of his life any longer." Greg stared hard at his ex-wife. "But if you want to be part of his life, then as long as you're sincere, I'm happy with that."

Joyce smiled slightly and nodded.

"However, you have to win Davey over, and that is going to be akin to climbing Mt. Kilimanjaro. He doesn't want to see you and has made it clear to me that he has no intention of going anywhere with you. So if you want a relationship with him, then you're going to have to show Davey that's what you want, and you're going to have to earn his forgiveness." Greg shook his head. "I can't imagine that will be an easy task. He's hurt, and that hurt has been festering for a while. He's been through a lot in the past year, so you're going to have to be gentle."

Joyce stood and stared through the windows into the backyard. Davey and Skip sat at the table with Davey waving his hands and talking what looked like a mile a minute. "What do I do?" she asked, and then she swallowed hard. "You know I was never very good with kids."

"Davey isn't a kid. He's a young man who's done a lot of growing up in the past year. It's up to you, Joyce. If you decide you don't want a relationship with him and are only here to somehow take over decision-making so you can seem like you're doing something, then go now, because that he doesn't need. Otherwise, he's out there." Greg pointed, and Joyce seemed unsure of what she was going to do. "Those are your only choices."

"I don't know what to say to him," Joyce said.

"I can't help you there," Greg said. "Just talk to him." He waited, and Joyce turned and walked toward the sliding glass doors. When she slid it open, Greg could hear Davey's animated voice drift inside. It cut off instantly, and Joyce shut the door. Greg turned his gaze to Sanjay, who shifted uncomfortably.

"I can't believe you'll stand in the way of possible help for your son," Sanjay began, and Greg threw him a gaze that froze him midsentence.

"You don't get to say anything like that to him," Tom said. "Greg is an amazing father."

Greg patted Tom's hand. "Davey has a doctor, and whatever you propose would be coordinated through him. I'm not allowing my ex-wife's fling to be a direct part of Davey's health care. That isn't going to happen. If Davey's regular ophthalmologist believes what you propose has merit, then he'll contact you and make any arrangements." Greg's anger was starting to get the best of him. How dare this guy insinuate that he didn't have Davey's best interests at heart?

"Are you even licensed to practice medicine in this state?" Tom asked.

"No. The procedures would be completed in Florida," Sanjay said.

"Well, you can forget that," Greg blurted and then forced himself to calm down. "But like I said, if you truly believe you can possibly help Davey, then I'll give you the name of his doctor and you can speak to him. If he believes the idea has merit, then I'll consider it." That was all Greg was willing to do. Sanjay gave him the creeps. If the treatment did have promise, then they'd find someone else to perform it.

The glass door slid open, and Skip came inside.

"What's going on?" Tom asked.

"It's like the ice queen meets Mr. Freeze out there. They're talking, but she has no idea what to say, and the kid isn't interested in talking to her, so they're spending most of their time sitting at the table, staring at each other. Which is probably a little weird, considering Davey can't see her." Skip flopped down into one of the chairs. "This has to be the coolest ranch house I've ever seen."

"Greg's an architect, and he designed the remodel," Tom said. "He's amazing. He did some work for people my family knows. Actually, he's quite well known."

Skip tilted his head to the side slightly and smiled. Greg wondered what that was all about.

"That's Skip's way of saying he thinks I'm being cute." Tom flashed Skip the finger, and he laughed.

"Would anyone like something to drink?" Greg asked and got up. "Sanjay, what can I get you?"

"Wine or beer is fine," he answered.

"Beer is fine for us," Tom said, and Greg went into the kitchen. As he passed the windows, he saw Davey and Joyce. It didn't look like any sort of thaw had happened. He sighed, went into the kitchen, and pulled bottles of beer out of the refrigerator. He got an opener and glasses, put them on a tray, and carried them back to the living area.

"Sanjay," Greg said as he opened two bottles, "would you take one to Joyce? And while you're there, tell her to ask Davey about playing beep ball. I told her a little about it on the phone. It might help break the ice." He handed the beers to him, and Sanjay stood and headed out toward the back.

"That was really nice," Tom whispered as he opened the remaining bottles and filled glasses.

"No one should go through life thinking their mother doesn't like them. That's just not right. I know Davey wants her attention, but he's too hurt to admit it. So if he can get over some of that hurt, it's good. They'll probably never be super close unless she makes a great deal of effort, though I don't see that happening, but Davey knowing his mother in some way is better than him thinking the worst of her."

Greg sat back down next to Tom and every now and then stood so he could see out. From the way they were sitting, it seemed the thaw had come, at least a little. They were talking, and after a few minutes Sanjay came back inside and joined them.

"That was a nice thing you did," he said. "That broke the ice and they're talking. Davey is telling her all about this game, and he even said she could come watch tomorrow if she wanted."

Greg smiled. "So what did you guys do today?" he asked Skip.

"Tom took me around town. It's nice. I was expecting something smaller. We saw the lake, and he said that while I'm here, he'll show me the sights in the area. Apparently there are waterfalls, and I saw a sign for something called Pictured Rocks. And I guess I'm playing beep baseball tomorrow. Tom said he has a blindfold I can use." Skip laughed.

"I wasn't kidding. We need more players for the team. You know what baseball is, so you can play. And afterwards we'll go out for pizza."

"Har har," Skip said before drinking from his glass. "So what is there to do for fun around here?"

"Skip, this is it. There aren't high-end clubs and fancy gourmet restaurants like in New York."

"Not even one?" Skip asked in complete disbelief.

"No. Life here is more basic and less frantic. We're joining them for dinner and then maybe we'll come back and have a drink and talk. Early tomorrow evening, we're playing beep baseball with Davey."

"What time do you go to bed?" Skip asked before taking another drink.

Greg looked at Tom. "About ten or so." Greg thought Skip was going to do a spit take. He glanced at Tom, wondering what he'd given up to move here, and if he would eventually get bored and want to move back to New York. Life here was nothing like that, and if that pace and activity was what he was used to, then hell, maybe Tom would get bored with him.

"Good God. Do you sleep your lives away?" Skip asked, looking at all of them, but centering on Tom.

"No. We go to bed at a reasonable hour. Besides, when was the last time you were actually out of bed before noon? You sleep the entire morning away every day," Tom teased. "Tomorrow morning it's going to take a crowbar to get him out of bed at a reasonable hour."

"No, it's not. I had to be up early to catch my flight. I'll probably be tired," Skip said. "And I don't go out every night, just most nights," he added sheepishly.

"How did you and Skip meet each other?" Sanjay asked.

"We went to college together, and after we graduated, we remained friends and stayed in New York," Tom said and then turned toward Greg. "Skip and I were never anything more than friends, though. We used to go clubbing together and pick up guys. Sometimes we tried for the same one. God, that was bad, especially when the guy in question wasn't interested in either of us." Tom began to laugh, and Skip laughed right along with him.

"That was so embarrassing," Skip said.

"And dumb. Were we delusional? I remember telling each other we were going to meet someone really interesting, but all we ever saw were barflies. Turned out we saw the same guys over and over again. After a while it got really dull," Tom said.

"Things have changed. There are so many new clubs now," Skip said.

"With the same guys, looking for the same things they always have, just in a different setting. I like it here. People are real and don't play games." Tom took Greg's hand, and they shared a smile.

"If you two get any sweeter, I'm going to need a dentist," Skip quipped.

Greg wasn't sure how to take that, but Tom laughed it off.

"There's nothing wrong with being happy. You should try it," Tom said and then stood up. "I'm going to go out back. I need to stretch my legs."

"Why don't we all go?" Greg suggested. "There are plenty of chairs, and it's a nice day to be outside." Sanjay didn't look convinced, but Greg was dying to find out how things were going between Davey and Joyce. They all followed him through the living area to the door, which he slid open, letting everyone outside. Once they were settled, Greg went back inside for a second round of beers, along with a Coke for Davey, before sitting next to Tom on the wicker settee.

"Did you and your mom have a good talk?" Greg asked Davey.

"Yeah," Davey said with just a hint of enthusiasm. "I explained beep ball to her, and she's going to come tomorrow to watch me play."

Joyce turned toward him, and Greg nodded once. Then he checked his watch and settled back in the chair. By all rights, he should be nervous and jittery. He was sitting on his back patio with his ex-wife and her... whatever Sanjay was... and his boyfriend—he liked the way that sounded in his mind—and Skip, along with a slightly confused Davey, who seemed to be trying to follow the conversations.

"Davey, Skip is going to play beep ball with you tomorrow too, and we may have some other players."

"Are any of them like me?" Davey asked.

"I hope so," Tom said.

"Remember, your teacher might come as well," Greg said. "It seems there are lots of people who find this curious, so we might have more spectators than players."

"Interest is interest, and it all helps in gaining support," Tom explained.

"Are you hoping to be able to play games?" Joyce asked. "I mean, what if he gets hurt?"

"I'm fine, Mom," Davey said. "Dad is there, Uncle Tom is there, and so are Uncle Howard and Uncle Gordy. They make sure I'm safe. Well, not Uncle Howard. He's blind like me, but he has Token and he says they're the team mascots." Davey stood and moved over to where Greg sat. Greg moved a chair next to him and helped Davey into it. Joyce passed over the can of soda, and Greg placed it in Davey's hands.

"Davey was really good in Little League," Greg said. "I think I sent you some of his team pictures," he added to Joyce, who nodded.

"The whole purpose of the game is to open up another avenue to people who are visually challenged," Tom chimed in. "There are leagues and even a World Series."

"There must be special equipment," Sanjay said.

"Yes. Tom got all that. We have everything we need except players, and we're hoping to have those soon," Greg said, taking Tom's hand. "It isn't so much about playing games and winning as it is about having interesting and challenging activities for people who can't see. We even went out to eat afterward, just like other teams do." He didn't mention that they'd gone to Tom's house and had frozen tacos. That wasn't important. What he was trying to get across was that anything that made Davey feel as though he'd lost less because of his blindness was a good thing, and he was going to support it, no matter what. "You had a good time, didn't you, Davey?"

"Yup, and we're going to play again tomorrow, right?" Davey asked Tom.

"As long as it isn't raining, we're going to play tomorrow. Skip and I will meet you and your dad at the park at seven. I'll bring the equipment, and we'll play. Sophia is going to join in, as is Hanna. They all want to get in on the act and have some fun. I've been contacted by other people who might be interested, so we might get lucky. We'll have to see." Tom settled against him, and the conversation moved on for a while.

Greg checked his watch a few times as they talked. This experience was more than a little surreal, sitting on his deck with his ex-wife and actually hoping she and Davey could repair some of the hurt between them, for Davey's sake.

"You okay?" Tom whispered when it was nearly time for them to leave for dinner.

"I'll tell you later," Greg said as he set his half-empty bottle aside. He noticed that Tom hadn't had much of his drink either. Skip, on the other hand, seemed to be having a good time.

When it was time to leave, Greg provided Joyce and Sanjay with directions to the restaurant. Tom asked Davey if he wanted to ride with him, so Greg drove Skip in his car, following the Ferrari, with Joyce and Sanjay following him. They made for an interesting convoy. Davey was all smiles when he got out of the Ferrari at the restaurant. Greg had called ahead, and they easily got a table.

Dinner was nice. Well, as nice as could be expected. Davey sat next to him and talked with everyone but his mother and Sanjay, except to answer their direct questions. It was upsetting Joyce, but there was nothing Greg could do about it. She needed to be the one to make the effort, and while he was willing to help give them a little boost, that was all he could do. The rest was up to them.

"So you really think you can help Davey?" Tom asked Sanjay toward the end of the meal.

"I can try," Sanjay answered, and Greg liked him a little more. If he'd have made lofty promises, Greg could easily have dismissed him. But he didn't.

"Sanjay is going to contact Dr. Jerry, and they'll discuss things," Greg told Davey.

"I might be able to see again?" Davey asked, hope instantly springing up. Greg looked sternly at Sanjay.

"We don't know, Davey. Your dad has asked that I work with your doctor to see if it's possible. There's nothing more to it right now," Sanjay replied.

"Davey, we've already seen a lot of doctors, and they've ruled out all the available treatments they know about. This could be one of those. It could also be something new, and if it is, then you and I will decide together if we want to take the chance. I promise you that." They'd ridden this roller coaster of hope again and again only to have it speed downhill and come to nothing. Greg didn't want this to be another of those times.

"I know, Dad," Davey said softly, and Greg's heart ached. He placed his arm around Davey's shoulder to comfort him, and alternately looked at the faces around the table. Joyce dabbed her eyes with a tissue, and even Sanjay looked moved. He didn't have to look at Tom to know how he felt, but when he did, he saw nothing but support. Skip looked like he was trying to figure out what was happening.

Thankfully, the server brought the check and Greg paid it. Then everyone stood to leave.

"Will I be able to see Davey tomorrow?" Joyce asked him.

"He has class, and I have to go into the office. We'll have a quick dinner and then go to the park. So why don't you meet us there? We plan to go for pizza afterward, and you can join us if you want," Greg explained. Joyce looked miffed. "I did explain that we had appointments and schedules that have to be kept."

She huffed slightly and then her expression brightened a little.

"I'll call Davey's doctor in the morning and ask him to contact you," Greg told Sanjay and took the card he offered.

"Bye, Davey, I'll see you tomorrow," Joyce said.

Greg could tell she was waiting for a hug, but Davey didn't move. She stepped forward, and Greg shook his head, hoping she wouldn't force the issue. She took his hand instead and held it for a few seconds, then released it and walked away.

"Do you want to come back to the house?" Greg offered.

Skip yawned rather dramatically. "Tom, why don't you take me back to your place? I can relax for a while, and you can spend time with Greg."

Tom paused. "Are you sure?"

"Of course I am," Skip said, pushing open the restaurant door. He held it, and they all walked outside. Greg guided Davey to the car, and they rode home in near silence.

"You know, it's okay for Tom to spend the night," Davey said. Greg nearly drove off the road. "I know about the birds and the bees. You like Tom, and he likes you. It's okay if you wanna do the dance with no pants."

"Davey, where did you hear that?"

"Television," he answered giggling. "That is how you feel about Tom, isn't it?"

"I like Tom a lot and…." Greg swallowed hard. He could not believe he was talking about this with his son. He was too young, and…. But Davey was growing up, and he needed to understand that.

"Do you like Tom or *like* Tom?" Davey asked.

"I... this... this is something I'd rather talk about with him," Greg finally answered.

"*Okay*," he agreed dramatically and then grew quiet, to Greg's everlasting relief. "Do you think I'll be gay because you're gay?"

"You'll be who you are, and I'll love you no matter what," Greg answered, relieved about the comparatively easy question.

"Do you think Mom would hate me if I'm gay?" Davey asked.

"I think your mother will love you no matter what."

"Why doesn't she love me now?" Davey retorted. "She's being all friendly because she wants something. I just haven't figured out what it is."

Greg cringed, because that was almost exactly what he'd said about Joyce. He had to remember to be more careful about what Davey heard. "What if all she wants is to be a part of your life?" Greg asked gently. "She seemed to genuinely care."

"But only because I'm blind," Davey said with the now familiar arms-over-his-chest move.

Greg made the turn onto their street and pulled into the drive. "Sometimes it takes something bad happening before people realize what they have or could have lost." Davey shrugged, and Greg continued. "You can't see anymore, and neither of us is happy about that. But as a parent, we keep running through the worse things that could have happened." Greg took a deep breath, his emotions close to the surface. "See, what if something had happened and you weren't here anymore? That's what really scares me."

"Being blind scares me," Davey said.

"I know, it scares me too, but the idea of not having you with me scares me even more." Greg turned off the engine and undid his seat belt. Davey did the same and opened his door. He picked up the cane he'd placed at his feet.

"I hate this thing," Davey said, getting out of the car. Greg got out as well and hurried around to where Davey was. He wanted to hug him, hold him tight, and never let him go. That way he couldn't get hurt. Of course, he couldn't do that, and Davey would inevitably get hurt, probably more than once.

"How did they tell you to use it?" Greg asked.

Davey moved the cane out in front and lightly swept back and forth, tapping the ground. "It still feels weird," Davey said. Just then the cane slipped off the pavement and onto the grass. Davey adjusted where he was walking and made it around the car, moving toward the front walk. "I get how to use it. I just don't like it." Davey threw the cane to the ground. "I want to see again, Dad."

Greg picked up the cane and remained quiet.

Davey stood still and shook. "Do you hear me? I want to see again!"

"Yes, I hear you. But I don't know if anyone can make that happen." Greg ached to give Davey what he wanted. Every parent wanted to give their child the best they could. But Greg was helpless, because what Davey wanted was outside his power to give.

"Dr. Sanjay said...."

"He said there was a possible treatment that might work to restore some of your sight," Greg said. "That's a lot of maybes, mights, and hopefullys. What if it doesn't happen, Davey? You've already seen specialists." Greg stepped to Davey, hugging him close. "I don't want you disappointed for nothing." Greg closed his eyes and felt Davey take hold of him. "What if they are able to get your sight back and then it goes away again? I don't know what's possible any longer."

"But, Dad...."

"Davey, I know how you feel, and I want the same thing. If I think there's any real hope, then you and I will sit down and talk about it, I promise, from the bottom of my heart. You and I will make the decision together. But you can't stop taking classes and using the tools you have." Greg pressed the cane back into Davey's hand. "Now, you're almost at the walk. You can make it to the front door." He was pushing, he knew that, and he wondered if he was doing the right thing as Davey slowly navigated the walk and up the step. Greg unlocked the door and waited for Davey to go inside.

Greg was about to follow when he heard a powerful car approaching. Tom's Ferrari appeared and then turned into the drive. Greg waited while Tom put up the top. Tom then got out and approached. Without a word, he pulled Greg into a hug. "What is it?"

"Nothing. Davey's just frustrated. He wants what he wants, but I can't give it to him."

"I'm sorry for bringing it up at dinner. I should have kept my mouth shut," Tom apologized.

"It wasn't your fault. I'm aware that Davey most likely heard us talking earlier, even while he was in his room. You warned me there would be times like this, and it's happening now." Greg let himself be held; it was what he needed.

CHAPTER
Eight

TOM LOVED holding Greg and would do it all day if he could. "Where's Davey now?" he whispered.

"Inside," Greg answered, but he didn't move away. "He hates his cane and threw it on the ground."

Tom nodded. "He's going to direct his anger either at you or what he sees as the trappings of his blindness." Tom slowly moved them toward the house. "You take care of Davey, but who takes care of you?"

"I'm fine," Greg said. "I think I'm actually holding up really well, considering…."

"So do I," Tom whispered. They went inside, and Tom closed the door, then looked around and pressed Greg against it. "But I would like a much closer inspection just to be sure."

Greg stilled. "Davey asked if we were together that way."

"Well, after he goes to bed, why don't you and I go into your bedroom and see what happens?"

"I'm not really a 'see what happens' kind of guy. Not with Davey, and…."

Tom kissed him to cut off his words. They were replaced by a small, needy moan.

"What I meant was, we'll spend some time together and let things take their course. No plans, no expectations, no worries—just you and me. For a few hours, we can leave the rest of the world outside the door."

Greg stilled and locked their gazes. "A few hours?"

Tom sighed. "Oh, yeah. I intend to take all the time in the world with you. You're worth every second, and if no one has ever treated you that way, then you haven't been with the right guys. And I intend to do everything I can to change that." Tom kissed him with intent, and Greg shook slightly. Then Tom backed away with a smile, looking down at himself to make sure he wasn't too obscene. Greg did the same thing, and Tom grinned when he turned away slightly.

"Dad, can we have ice cream?"

"Of course we can," Greg answered rather loudly. "I have chocolate and mint chip here, is that okay?" He really wasn't particularly interested in going out for ice cream, but he'd do what Davey wanted.

"I want chocolate," floated to their ears as an answer.

"Do you want ice cream?" Greg asked. "I can get some for all of us."

"Sure," Tom said with a grin. This seemed so normal. His family never did simple things like this.

"You have to come out to the deck," Greg called to Davey and then headed to the kitchen. "In case you haven't guessed, the world's most efficient form of birth control is children."

Tom laughed. "Hey, it doesn't matter. What does is that once he's in bed, you're all mine."

Greg pulled the ice cream out of the freezer.

"I'm thinking of some interesting things we could do with that ice cream."

Greg stopped and wagged the spoon at him. "Don't even think about it. I tried fun with food once—it was messy and it took three washings to get the chocolate syrup stains out of the sheets. They must have a huge cleanup budget in porn, because in real life, that's just a mess." Greg smiled and got dishes out of the cupboard. "What do you want? I have strawberry too, but Davey doesn't like it."

"Mint chip is fine. It will give me fresher breath for later," Tom teased.

Davey came down the hall and made his way around the furniture toward the deck.

"Some of the chairs were moved. Be careful out there," Greg said.

"I will," Davey answered and went out. Tom watched and saw him sit in the first chair he encountered. Greg finished dishing out the ice cream. Tom carried the bowls while Greg got drinks and followed behind. Out on the deck, Tom set the bowls on the table and handed Davey his along with a napkin.

"I won't make a mess," Davey said.

"Didn't say you would," Tom said, wondering where that came from.

"I heard Mom whisper to Sanjay at dinner that I was making a mess." Davey scowled into his bowl and then carefully began to eat.

"She isn't used to being around you and doesn't know how hard it is to learn something new like that." Tom smiled as an idea struck him. He'd have to talk with Greg about it later. Joyce's comment struck him as wrong, and they needed to do something about it. Greg joined them and sat next to Tom on the settee. "It's really nice out here."

"Sometimes it can get chilly once the sun goes down, but the air is still, so the lake doesn't have a chance to cool things off too much."

"Did you get along with your mother otherwise?" Tom asked Davey.

He shrugged. "I guess. She's so uptight and worried about how things look. She actually asked me if I picked out my own clothes. I think she thought I didn't match or something." Davey continued eating, and Tom turned to Greg. He mouthed that he'd tell him later.

"Don't be too hard on your mother. I don't think she means to be bitchy. She just doesn't know how to act or what to say," Tom said, and Davey nearly snorted ice cream through his nose. Tom handed him another napkin and took Davey's bowl as he doubled over with laughter.

"Davey, that's enough."

"But Tom said...."

"I know what Tom said, and if you want to be treated as anything other than a kid, then you need to act like it. He wasn't calling your mother a bitch, he said she was *being* bitchy, and she probably was. So if you can't behave, we'll start censoring what we say around you."

Davey straightened up, and Tom handed him his bowl. "Now, as I was saying. I don't think she means to act that way. She doesn't know any different."

"If you say so," Davey said, returning to his ice cream. "I still think she was mean."

"Ignorant and a little scared isn't the same as mean."

Davey stopped. "She was scared... of what?"

"You, probably," Tom said. He looked at Greg, who nodded, so he turned back to Davey. "Being around you is going to make some people uncomfortable. Sometimes they'll pass by and hope you don't notice. Others will try to start a conversation, but not know what to say. They might want to talk and they'll be curious, but they won't want to ask about being blind because it makes them uncomfortable or they think it's rude. That could be what's happening with your mother. Just give her a little time."

Davey didn't seem convinced.

"She must have done something right—you invited her to come tomorrow," Greg said.

"Yeah, well." Davey began eating in earnest, and they left him alone.

"Are you designing anything interesting?" Tom asked Greg.

"I've got a builder who bought a number of properties at auction and he wants to remodel them into higher-end places. So I'm redesigning the interiors, opening them up, like I did here. One of the homes has a great dining area, so after opening it up, we're adding crystal chandeliers throughout the entire space. The buyer has a collection of Venetian mirrors, so we're going to use them to reflect the sparkle. It should be quite an effect."

"That sounds so cool," Tom said.

"Think Versailles in miniature. A little light should go a long way and create an incredibly warm space because of the old glass. I'm also doing an ultramodern interior. I'm not sure how that will go over, but it was what he asked for. I'm holding something a little more traditional in reserve just in case, though. How about you?"

"Nothing new with me. I have to go down to Grand Rapids in a few weeks for a foundation board meeting." Tom rolled his eyes. "They talk themselves to death and say nothing at all. But it's a necessary evil. The worst part is that many of the people on the board are family members with their own agendas, old hurts, and alliances."

"A political minefield," Greg offered.

"Yes and no. They may squabble, but when I came on board, I made sure I had real authority." Tom grinned. "Besides, I'm good at what I do. The foundation does very well because of me, and they know it. People have said I should open my own investment firm, but that isn't what I'm interested in. I like the investing thing, don't get me wrong, but turning it into a full-time job would suck the fun out of it, and then I wouldn't have the time for the other things I want to do."

"Like what?" Greg asked, setting his bowl aside.

"I have some ideas floating around right now, but they haven't settled just yet," Tom answered. "I always get what I think are great ideas, but over time most of them don't pan out for one reason or another. Right now I'm working with the parks department again on a project for trail refurbishment. But those kinds of things are pretty small."

"They're important," Greg said. "People always want to think big, but it's the small things that can make a difference. In that house with all the mirrors, they have to be hung and it isn't like they can just put nails in the walls. I designed a method to hang the mirrors so they can be placed and easily moved later. The mirrors will be attached by a small hook which will fix to the pin and holder. If that little piece of metal isn't strong enough, it won't hold the mirrors. The entire effect we're going for rests on that one single piece. So, yeah, I understand about thinking big, but don't discount the little things."

"I see your point," Tom said.

Greg shifted his attention to Davey. "If you're done, then put your dish on the counter and get ready for bed. You have class tomorrow, and beep ball tomorrow night."

"Okay," Davey answered and stood up. Tom watched as Davey went inside. He carried the bowl in one hand and used the other to feel his way.

"Night, Davey," Tom called after him.

"I'll be in to say good night in a few minutes," Greg added before Davey shut the door.

"He's learning to get around very well."

"Yes," Greg said and then shifted on the seat. "You know I'd do anything for Davey to be able to see again."

Tom stilled. "Where did that come from?"

"I keep thinking about what Sanjay said about helping Davey see again, and I'm wondering if I dismissed what he had to say because he was with Joyce. What if he really could help Davey see again?"

"And what if he's only offering false hope?" Tom asked. "For what it's worth, I think you did the right thing. Let Davey's doctor look into it and evaluate what Sanjay is proposing. He'll have access to resources you don't. It isn't as though you discounted him completely. You were cautious, and I can't blame you for that. No one can, not even Sanjay." Tom paused a second. "There's nothing at all wrong with being cautious."

"Thanks," Greg said softly, not sounding convinced.

"Don't second-guess your instincts. Chances are they're spot-on."

Greg smiled and stood up. "I need to say good night to Davey. I shouldn't be long."

Greg left, and Tom settled on the seat, looking over the yard and imagining he could hear the sound of the waves on the lake. They were probably too far away, but sometimes he swore he could hear the constant waves on the shore. Tom closed his eyes and let his mind drift. When he heard the door slide open again, he didn't open them and waited. Nothing happened. He knew Greg was nearby from his soft breathing, but other than that, he didn't hear a sound.

Greg caressed his cheek, softly and gently. Tom held still, keeping his eyes closed, and let Greg have free rein. "You're so...."

"What?" Tom whispered.

"Perfect," Greg answered. "I can't figure out what I did to catch your attention. You have everything, and I'm just... ordinary."

Tom leaned forward and wrapped his arms around Greg, pulling him closer. "You aren't ordinary. I've seen what ordinary looks and acts like, and believe me, you're nothing like it. The way you are with Davey is extraordinary, believe me, and every time I'm with you I feel special. No one has ever made me feel that way." Tom rested his head against Greg's chest, hearing his heart beating. "I've had lots of guys want to be with me, guys who wanted me for my money, or what they thought I could do for them, but not you." Tom lifted his gaze, and Greg kissed him lightly, cupping his cheeks.

"Let's go inside," Greg whispered. He moved away, holding Tom's hand.

Tom stood and followed Greg inside, then closed the door behind them. The house was dark and quiet.

"I used to leave a light on for Davey…," Greg said as they passed through the living room. Greg led him down the hall, past Davey's room, which was dark and silent, to the final door on the left. They went inside, and Greg closed the door behind them. Then he stilled in the dimly lit room. There was just enough light for Tom to see the outline of the bed and dresser. "I'm not sure what to do," Greg whispered. "I've been with guys before… but not in a while, and no one I've ever…."

"Ever what…?" Tom prompted.

"No one I've ever wanted to make love with," Greg said, and Tom took him in his arms, held Greg tight, and kissed him with all the joy in his heart. Greg vibrated slightly in his arms, energy sizzling between them. "Tom, I'm nervous," Greg whispered once he broke the kiss.

"Why? All you have to do is be you."

"But what if that isn't good enough?" Greg asked.

"It's more than good enough," Tom said. "It's perfect."

Greg laughed, and Tom stilled. He'd been trying to be romantic and didn't understand Greg's reaction.

"I'm sorry. I'm far from perfect; I know that."

"Neither of us is perfect, but that's the beauty of love."

"Where did you hear that?" Greg asked.

"From my grandfather. He always said that alone, he couldn't have done anything. It was Grandma who gave him the drive and the support he needed to build the business. He said she made up for all his faults. Once he said he brought her to a bank meeting so she could charm a loan officer who drove him crazy. He said Grandma had him eating out of her hand in a few minutes, and he got what he wanted without any of the fuss and drama he would have had to go through. See, Grandpa could be pushy and impatient with people, and Grandma was quiet and had the patience of a saint." Tom lightly stroked Greg's cheek. "What Grandpa told me was that in this world, if you're lucky, you get a chance to meet the person who's the other half of your soul. He said that Gram was that person for him."

"Okay, but...."

"He told me that Gram wasn't perfect, just perfect for him." Tom smoothed his thumb over Greg's lower lip and then leaned in closer. Greg stilled, and Tom kissed him.

Together they moved toward the bed. Tom pressed Greg back against it and then down. He continued kissing, taking all the time in the world. Greg moaned softly and clutched at his shoulders. "But how do you know?"

Tom paused. "Do you really want to talk about this now?" Greg was quiet for a few seconds. "All Grandpa ever told me when I asked him was that I would know when it happened, just the way he did with Gram." Tom smiled and hoped Greg could see it. He waited to see if Greg had any more questions. He didn't seem to, so Tom leaned close, inhaling deeply, taking in Greg's rich scent. He nuzzled the base of Greg's neck and then kissed him. Salty richness assaulted his taste buds, and he kissed and tasted. "Damn, you smell good," he whispered.

"So do you," Greg whimpered.

Tom kissed Greg hard, reached for the tail of his shirt, and pulled it out of Greg's pants. Then he slid his hand up under the fabric. Greg was hot and smooth. Tom loved the way the muscles quivered under his touch. "Is this what you want?" Tom asked.

"Yes. It's been a long time since I was touched like that," Greg whispered, but the tightness in his voice stilled Tom's hand.

"Do you want me to stop?" Tom asked.

"No," Greg whimpered. "Like I said, I'm nervous and...."

"Hey," Tom whispered. "There's nothing at all to be nervous about, I promise you that. Close your eyes for me and take a deep breath... good... now release it slowly." As Greg did, Tom made small circles on his belly. "Let yourself go with the feelings inside." He made larger circles and moved up to Greg's chest, ghosting his fingertips over Tom's nipples. "I know it's been a while, and I know you have a million things on your mind, but let it all go. For right now, there's only you and me. The world is outside and it can't get in. So don't worry or give anyone a care except you." Tom lifted Greg's shirt. Now that his eyes had adjusted, he could see Greg fairly well. He shifted slightly and licked across Greg's chest, then sucked gently on a nipple. Some guys didn't like that, but Greg certainly did, judging by the chorus of soft moans that filled the room.

Greg stretched out, and Tom held him still, exposing as much skin as possible. He kissed and licked down Greg's flat belly and up his side, then teased a nipple before capturing Greg's lips.

"Tom, please...."

"I told you I was going to take my time, and I am." He tugged at Greg's shirt and managed to get it over his head. Tom ignored his own need and the tightness in his pants in favor of taking in everything that was Greg. "Scooch up on the bed," he whispered. He let Greg get comfortable, then he straddled Greg's legs and began a massage he hoped would drive Greg wild.

He started at Greg's shoulders and neck, stroking lightly because he didn't have any oil. Then down his arms to Greg's hands, lifting each in turn, caressing each finger before returning to Greg's shoulders. Greg's chest was next for stroking, touching, and definitely teasing. This type of massage wasn't meant to relax, but to heighten sensation. His hope was to make Greg's skin sing and heighten his arousal, and from the way Greg's muscles throbbed beneath his hands and the way he quivered whenever Tom paused, it was working. When he got to Greg's belly, the muscles tensed and trembled rapidly. Greg held his breath, and Tom knew exactly what Greg was doing. "Are you praying I'll go farther?"

"Uh-huh," Greg answered breathlessly.

"Like this?" Tom asked and ran his fingers under the waistband of his pants. Greg shifted his hips, and Tom smiled at the prominent bulge. He did it again, and Greg thrust his hips upward as best he could, whimpering softly.

"Tom," Greg whined.

Tom chuckled softly and opened Greg's belt, pulled it off, and let it settle to the floor. Greg was wound tighter than a drum and getting more excited by the second. The energy in the room ramped up higher and higher. Tom had been with lots of guys, some longer than others, but he'd never encountered this kind of sexual excitement—and they both still had most of their clothes on. "I promised you that I would take my time, and I want you to know, without any doubt, what I feel for you. This isn't some quick fuck or a fast time. As you said, this is making love, and I think it's about time someone did it all the way for you." He leaned forward to kiss Greg and heard a thump from outside the room.

Greg stilled and they both listened, neither of them moving. The sound didn't come again and there was nothing further.

"I should check on Davey," Greg said.

Tom nodded and shifted off Greg's legs. He watched as Greg slid off the bed and walked toward the door. He opened it and left the room. This was so not how he'd expected or wanted this to go. He'd planned this and had wanted to drive Greg wild, but that required an erotic spell, which now had been broken.

Greg came back inside and closed the door behind him. "Davey banged the headboard. He didn't even wake up." He made his way back toward the bed. "He's becoming more active when he sleeps, thrashing and kicking off the covers." Greg sat back down on the side of the mattress. "I'm sorry. I know this ruined everything, but I had to make sure he was okay."

"Of course you did," Tom said, trying to keep any hint of his frustration out of his voice. He knew Greg was right, but he'd also wanted his undivided attention for just a few hours.

Greg shifted and turned, moving closer. "He should sleep the rest of the night," Greg whispered. "I'll understand if...."

Tom didn't move for a split second. Then he pulled Greg to him and kissed him hard. "You're a father," he said.

"Yeah...."

Tom didn't let him go. "I mean... I'm basically a selfish person. I'm used to being the center of attention, either because of what I have or with the people in my life. But I can't be the center of your attention because that's Davey, and it will always be Davey."

"He's my son."

"I know." Tom took a second to get his thoughts together. "I'm not saying it's a bad thing, or wrong, just something I need to get used to."

"Is it something you're willing to live with? I can't not care for Davey or put him on a shelf to pick up later because you and I want to do something or spend some time together. He needs me, and he will for a very long time."

Tom nodded and leaned close, touching Greg's lips with his. "I don't think I'd care for you as much as I do if you did put Davey aside for me or anyone." The words were out of his mouth before he could stop them. That was usually not like him. Yes, Tom was generous with many things, but he'd always required the undivided attention of his boyfriends. Hell, in most of his previous relationships, he'd been the one to call the shots. Maybe that was why the relationships had eventually ended. He didn't know for sure, but it was possible.

Greg kissed him, and Tom returned it, pulling them back on the bed. Greg entwined himself around him, pushing tightly against him. Tom pulled at his own shirt, breaking the kiss long enough to get it over his head. Then the kisses continued. The energy that had seemed to evaporate earlier came back quickly, and Tom realized it was because of both of them, together. Greg stroked up his back and then wound his fingers in his hair. Soft moans filled the room, only this time it wasn't just Greg, but both of them.

Tom tugged at Greg's pants, shifting for access and parting the fabric. Then he pressed them down over his hips.

They worked at each other's remaining clothes with increasing intensity. Pants, shoes, and socks all ended up strewn onto the floor. Tom's grand seduction had shifted to mutual passion. Eventually, Greg moved against him. Tom sighed when, chest to chest and hips to hips, they settled together. This was what he'd been waiting and hoping for.

"Tom," Greg whispered, arching his back and moving his hips slightly.

Tom rolled them on the bed, pressing Greg into the mattress, loving the skin-to-skin contact. He stroked Greg's cheek, nearly unable to contain the energy that coursed through him. "I know, I feel it too." Tom kissed Greg and then slid slowly downward, kissing a long wet trail over Greg's chest and then down his belly. Greg's cock bounced and jumped.

"Not gonna last too long," Greg whimpered.

Tom could tell and figured if that were the case he was going to go for the gold, so he opened his mouth and sucked Greg hard and deep.

Greg came unglued. It was the only way to describe it. He groaned loudly and stuck the ball of his hand in his mouth, breathing hard and letting himself go. Greg tasted exactly the way Tom thought he would—rich and tangy. He sucked hard, running his tongue around the head and then sucking him deeply once again. Tom stroked Greg's belly and then up to his chest to tweak his nipples. Greg seemed to become more excited, thrusting his hips as Tom moved.

"Tom, stop," Greg breathed after a few seconds. Tom paused and let Greg slip from between his lips. "I'm gonna come and I don't want to yet. It's way too soon, and I don't want it to stop...."

"It won't, I promise, but we can slow down a little if you like." He wasn't too sure how long either of them would last, but it didn't matter. Greg caressed down his back and over his butt, cupping his cheeks and then pressing up against Tom even more tightly. "I have a feeling that it's going to take quite a long time before I get enough of you," Tom whispered, and then he sucked slightly on his neck.

Greg moaned and writhed beneath him. To hell with slow. Tom wriggled down Greg's skin, licking and sucking his way over a heaving chest and rippling belly. Greg stilled, and Tom sucked him deep in one fluid movement, then bobbed his head and licked along Greg's length, his cock throbbing along Tom's tongue. Damn, Tom loved this sensation, and the rich and slightly bitter taste drove him on. Tom sucked faster and harder, and when Greg's breathing caught, he stilled. Tom knew Greg was close, so he doubled his efforts, wanting more than anything to see Greg come apart.

He didn't have to wait long. Greg tensed, moaned deeply, and shook slightly before starting to come. Greg gave Tom everything he had to give, his mouth hanging open and eyes slightly glazed.

Tom waited until Greg splayed on the bed. Then Tom let him slip from between his lips. The look of near complete wonder in Greg's eyes told him all he needed to know. Tom brought their lips together in a deep kiss that fueled his own denied passion. Greg's skin on his cock drove him wild. Tom clutched Greg to him, thrusting his hips with abandon, sliding his cock along Greg's warm, sweat-slick skin. Within seconds, pressure built from deep inside and he came hard between their bodies.

Neither of them moved for a long while. They breathed and held each other in a soft afterglow that seemed to go on and on, to Tom's delight. Eventually, Greg got up and hurried out of the room to the bathroom. He returned with a cloth and towel that they both used to clean up.

"Do you want me to go?" Tom asked. "I'll understand if you don't want me to be here when Davey gets up in the morning."

Greg finished with the cloth and placed it on the hamper before joining him in bed. "I think Davey would approve, actually. He asked me why I wasn't dating, and I think he would be thrilled to know we were serious about each other." Greg paused. "We are serious, aren't we? I mean, if this is just a sex thing, I can live with that, but I need you to tell me. Davey likes you, and I don't want him to get hurt. I think I can deal with it, but he's—"

Tom touched Greg's lips lightly with a finger. He sort of liked the babbling thing Greg had going, but he needed to set him straight. "Yes, I think what we have is serious, and no, I have no intention of purposely hurting either you or Davey. But you have to realize that I'm in this relationship with you. I care for Davey a lot, but the person who's stealing my heart is you." That was a hard admission for him, but one he felt was necessary. "I don't usually pour my heart out to anyone, but you've gotten around my defenses, and what surprises me is that I don't mind in the least. You're a good, kind man without an agenda, and I haven't met many of those." Tom pulled Greg to him, spooning to him, making slow circles on his belly. "I want to stay, Greg, very much."

Greg was quiet for quite a while. "I'm glad you're staying. And I…."

"You don't have to say anything you aren't ready for."

"I know." Greg rolled over. "I care for you too. These past few weeks have been hard for both of us, and you've been with us all the way."

Tom smiled and closed his eyes, kissed Greg lightly and then held him in his arms.

This was their first night together, and Tom didn't want it to end. He lay awake for a good hour, listening to Greg breathe and letting himself start to believe just how wonderful things could be.

"Are you still awake?" Greg asked in the darkness.

"Yes," Tom answered.

"Is something wrong?"

"No," Tom breathed. "I can't sleep because I'm not used to having someone in bed with me like this. I'm excited and happy."

"But that's good," Greg whispered.

"It is, but that's also when my previous attempts at a relationship blew up."

"Okay." Greg chuckled slightly. "There will be no blowing up or any other military-style endings to this relationship. Okay? So just relax and go to sleep." Greg pressed back against him, and Tom heard another chuckle. "I see why you can't sleep," Greg said and began moving his hips, sliding Tom's now throbbing dick along his butt.

"I was trying not to be too obvious," Tom whispered in Greg's ear, holding him tighter as he thrust his hips. Tom let his hands wander down Greg's belly and wrapped his fingers around Greg's cock. He slowly began to stroke, and Greg thrust his hips against him. "That's it, let yourself float on the sensation," Tom whispered and then sucked on Greg's ear. "I love the way you feel against me, but I love even more the way you shake with excitement when I touch you."

"I feel so selfish," Greg said.

"No. You're letting me give, and that's what I want. You need to be happy, and making you happy does the same for me." Tom stroked harder and thrust faster, and Greg pressed back against him in a silent plea for more. The bed shook slightly as they slowly moved together in a horizontal dance that wrapped Tom in warmth unlike anything he'd felt before. He knew when Greg was close—he could tell by his little panting breaths and desperate movements. Tom wasn't far off, his body tuning to Greg's. "Your little groans drive me wild," Tom whispered, playing Greg like an instrument, driving them both to a crescendo of desire that quickly burst around them in a flash of searing heat that tapered off into a warm, slow fade, and after a more involved cleanup than before, they settled back in bed, and this time, Tom did fall asleep.

FIRST THING in the morning, he kissed Greg good-bye and left the house. Tom needed to get home, and of course once he got there, he found a number of beer bottles on the coffee table and Skip sound asleep in the guest room. Tom figured he should be pleased he hadn't found Skip passed out on the sofa or asleep on the bathroom floor. Both were experiences he wasn't really willing to relive. Tom decided to let him sleep and went to his room. He got fresh clothes and went to the bathroom, where he cleaned up, showered, and then got dressed. When he came out, he was graced with Skip coming toward him, bleary-eyed and blinky, clad only in a pair of old gym shorts.

"When did you get home?"

"A little while ago," Tom answered, and Skip gave him a smile. "It was nice, thanks."

"No problem," Skip said and then yawned. "What's on the agenda for today?"

"I thought I'd take you to the falls, if you're up to it. It's over an hour's ride. I thought we could spend some time communing with nature before it's time to get back and play beep ball with Davey."

"You really like him, don't you?"

"Yeah, Davey's a great kid," Tom answered.

"I was talking about Greg," Skip said with a soft laugh, followed by a yawn. He scratched his butt and stepped toward the bathroom. "I'll get cleaned up and dressed, and then we can go." He closed the door, and Tom went to his room to finish dressing. Then Tom headed to the kitchen. He made coffee, which inevitably drew Skip downstairs. After grabbing a quick bite, they got in the Ferrari and headed out for the day.

"You know," Skip said as they drove, "I came here to try to convince you to give up this foolishness and come back to New York. Everyone misses you, including me, but you aren't going to come back, I know that now. For some unfathomable reason, you're actually happy here in the sticks."

"I like it. What's wrong with that?"

"Nothing. That's what I'm coming to understand. When you left, I kept figuring you'd get bored and come back. I mean, New York has everything, and this place very little. But I'm starting to understand that Marquette has something that makes you happy. I wish to God I knew what it was, because the thought of living here out in the middle of nowhere would push me off the deep end."

"You're so dramatic," Tom said. "It isn't as bad as all that here. People are friendly, and there's plenty to do. You just have to look harder and be willing to make your own fun. I'm part of the community and I can be productive here. I wasn't in New York." Tom paused. "Okay, honestly, I wish I could tell you why I like it here, but I do. And I think you might like it here if you gave it a chance." Tom waited for the inevitable denial. When it didn't come, he smiled and kept quiet.

They drove for a while, with Skip looking out the window at the passing scenery. He asked a few questions, and Tom did his best to supply the answers. Tom turned off the main road, then slowed as a large shape lumbered out of the trees. He pulled to a stop and heard Skip gasp, then say, "Is that a fucking bear?"

Tom grinned. "I don't know about the fucking part, but yeah, that's a black bear. We're about to enter the state park, and it's very wild. Most of Michigan was logged at one point or another, but large portions of the state park were preserved and set aside before that happened." Tom stopped at the ranger station, where the ranger on duty checked the state park sticker on the windshield, asked about the car with a huge grin and a touch of jealousy, and let him pass through. "I wish Greg could have come with us," Tom said.

Skip sighed. "You know, there was a time when I wished you had those kind of feelings for me."

Tom nearly missed the turn he was looking for, he was so shocked at the admission. "We were friends, best friends...." He didn't know what else to say.

"I know," Skip said, and then, after a quiet moment, he added, "I didn't want to mess that up."

Tom pulled into a parking spot and turned off the engine. "You could have said something." Tom started running through their history together like a movie running on super-fast-forward. "I guess I never thought of you that way. I mean, you were my friend, and it's pretty bad to jones on your friend."

"Yeah, well. I knew it wasn't meant to be when you left the city. While you were there I kept thinking I might have a chance, but you never looked at me that way, so I guess I…."

"Drowned your sorrows in a parade of men?" Tom teased.

"Don't flatter yourself," Skip said and opened his door. Tom did the same, and they got out. "I'm not heartbroken or anything. I was…. Let's talk about something else. I probably should have kept my big mouth shut instead of sounding like some tragic character from a romantic comedy."

Tom shook his head. "Come on. Let's go see some nature." He led the way along the path from the parking lot to the visitor center. They stopped inside to get some basic information before walking down the path through the woods, the roar of falling water mixing with the wind through the thick canopy overhead. He really did wish he could be here with Greg. Greg had told him once that Tahquamenon Falls was one of his and Davey's favorite places.

"The forest here is thousands of years old." He gazed into the stands of large, thick trees, leaning on the wooden railing that ran along the path. "You know what gets to me?" Tom asked, almost under his breath.

Skip stood next to him. "That Davey will never get to see this again?"

Tom nodded slowly. "You know me so well."

"Yeah, I do," Skip agreed. "And I know that boy and his father have both gotten under your skin. But I want to ask you something, and I don't want you to get mad." Tom turned toward him. "Is it Davey who is pulling on your heartstrings, or is it Greg?" Tom opened his mouth to respond, anger rising to the surface. Skip put up his hands. "I'm just asking because I know you and your causes sometimes. You get wound up in things, and I love you, ya know that. But they aren't a cause."

Tom took a deep breath and pushed away from the rail. Skip did the same, and they continued down the path in silence. The path wound through the woods, and the roar of the falling water got louder. Then they made a turn, and there they were, the large upper falls. The falls were spectacular—a wide expanse of water tumbling over a hundred feet, natural and unspoiled. Tom stopped and simply watched the way he always did when he came here. People moved past him to get closer, but Tom simply stared, taking in the entire scene, the wilderness, the river and then the falls. There was something about this place that spoke to his soul.

"Are you ready to move on?"

"Give me a minute, Greg," Tom said, "I mean, Skip," he corrected hastily, shaking his head to pull him out of the fantasy he'd been allowing himself to weave.

"I think I just got my answer," Skip muttered, and then he turned and started walking down the path.

Tom caught up, and they continued on until they got closer, walking right up to the top of the falls, where they watched the water as it approached the precipice and then tumbled over, shifting from clear dark to white frothing water in a split second.

"It's incredible," Skip said over the roar, with more animation that Tom had heard all day.

"Yeah," Tom agreed, nodding.

"I can feel the energy all around. It's like the air crackles with it."

Tom knew exactly what he meant. After a while, they started back along the path, with people passing them as they answered the call of the wild river.

"You know, I never meant to hurt you," Tom said as they approached the Ferrari, a group of kids gathered around it, eyes filled with longing and admiration. Tom opened his door and let the boys have a look inside. They wanted to know all the statistics, and he gladly provided the information. Then he and Skip got inside.

"You didn't hurt me," Skip said. "I hurt myself with my delusions, but honestly that was a while ago, and I'm over you. I think I needed to clear the air."

Tom nodded and said nothing. He didn't think Skip was telling the truth, but to call him on it would hurt his pride, so he kept silent as they drove to the lower falls.

They had lunch and then paid for a boat trip to the island, where they followed the path along the edge where the river ran over smaller falls right near the path. These weren't as grand as the upper falls, but the cascades over smaller drop-offs were no less inspiring. By the time they'd walked the loop trail around the island, they were both ready to head back. Tom rowed their boat across the lagoon and back to the boat landing.

"That was amazing," Skip told him as they climbed the path to the gift shop.

Skip looked through shelves of souvenirs while Tom tried to calculate how long it had been since the assortment of merchandise had changed. The entire place felt like something out of another age—coin purses and stuffed black bears—when everything was more innocent. Maybe that was the draw. Families came here on vacation to escape from the hustle and bustle of everyday life. Tom smiled as a young boy picked up one of the bears and turned to his dad, a smile breaking out when the father nodded.

"What's wrong?" Skip asked. "You're staring."

"Didn't mean to. Just thinking about crap." Wishing his dad would have done something so simple with him when he was that age. "Let's go back. We have to make sure everything is charged and ready for beep ball. Was there something you were interested in?"

Skip walked back through the store and returned with half a dozen T-shirts in various colors. "I need something to bring back to the guys, and they'll get a kick out of these." He paid, and then they walked back to the car, where another group of people surrounded it. Tom did the same routine as before, and then they headed home.

The sky clouded over as they approached town. "Davey will be disappointed if it rains."

Skip pulled out his phone and began checking things. "There's nothing on the radar, probably just clouds."

They pulled into the drive, and Tom put the car in the garage. Then he began gathering the equipment, making sure it was all charged before packing it in the trunk of the BMW. Once that was done, they hung out for a while and then headed over to the ball field.

Skip helped him set up, and by the time Greg pulled in with Davey, Tom was all smiles.

"Did you have a good day?" Greg asked as he got out of the car and Tom hurried over to him.

"Yes," Tom answered and then kissed him. "But that was still one of the highlights."

"Is everything ready?" Davey asked. He was so excited he could hardly stand still.

"Yes." Other cars pulled in. He recognized Howard and Gordy's car along with Ken and Patrick's and Joyce's rental, but others arrived as well. "We have everything set up." Greg guided Davey toward where they were going to play, and Tom went along with them.

"We got you some additional players," Howard said with a smile from where he held Gordy's arm.

"Excellent," Tom said and lifted his head. "Please join us by the foot of the stands, and I'll explain the game and what we'll be doing today."

The sighted walked over to the stands, while the new parents aided their blind children. It took a while, and Tom quickly realized things were going to happen more slowly than he'd anticipated. When they'd played with just Davey, things had gone relatively quickly.

"Welcome to beep baseball, or as Davey calls it, 'beep ball,'" Tom said once everyone had gathered. "We aren't here to play a game or for competition, at least not today. This is about fun. I'm Tom Spangler."

"Are you the coach?"

"No, I'm just the organizer. Greg"—he motioned—"is going to act as coach, but really we're here just to have fun. Since we have new faces, I think we should make introductions."

"I'm Marty Phillips, and this is my son Kurt."

"How old are you, Kurt?" Tom asked in a much quieter tone.

"Nine," Kurt said.

"Have you played baseball before?"

"Kurt was born blind," Marty answered for him, and Kurt turned toward him. "That isn't a problem, is it?"

"Goodness, no," Tom said. "All of us are learning, and we'll do it together." He was so excited, and Tom glanced at Greg, seeing some of his excitement coming back to him. He wanted to run over and hug him hard, because things seemed to be coming together. He turned to the other man who had come.

"I'm Frank Gardner, and this is Heather," he said.

"Hi," Heather said happily. "I'm really excited to play."

"She's a real baseball fan," Frank said.

"Have you played?" Tom asked.

"No. I listen to the games with Daddy," Heather said.

"When we heard about this through Howard, she was so excited." Frank paused. "This isn't just for boys, is it?"

"No. Certainly not," Tom answered Frank. "Hanna and Sophia are going to play as well. They'll use blindfolds."

Frank smiled and hugged Heather to him. Introductions continued, and then Tom explained the basic rules of the game before turning things over to Greg. Tom checked out the equipment while Greg explained that they were going to start with moving between the bases. They'd figured one skill at a time was best. Parents took places at the bases, and the kids took turns moving between them, just like Tom and Greg had done with Davey previously. With each success, the kids laughed. Heather was totally fearless, and after one trip back and forth, she ran between the bases with a burst of speed. Sophia and Hanna were the most tentative, which wasn't surprising.

"Do you want to work on hitting?" Greg asked. "I think Heather is so eager that if she connects with the ball, she'll hit it out of the park."

"I agree. Kurt is still reticent. I'd let him run the bases a few more times." Tom looked over at Joyce.

"What are you thinking?" Greg asked.

"Hanna," Tom called, and she pulled off her blindfold and ran over. "Would you be willing to help for a few minutes so I can borrow your blindfold?"

"Sure," she said, sounding a little relieved before handing him the blindfold. "It isn't as easy as I thought it would be. Sophia said the same thing."

Tom couldn't help hugging her. "You're both doing beautifully, and I'm... proud of both of you for trying. The others need that." Tom glanced at Joyce, then back at Heather. "Thank you for this. Now let's have a little fun."

Hanna looked up at him, probably wondering what he was talking about. Tom released her and walked to where Sanjay and Joyce were sitting. They'd been talking between themselves, and a few times he'd heard her whispered comments.

"Would you like to try?" he asked her, holding out the blindfold. This idea had been running through his mind since the day before. Tom made sure his tone came across with the hint of a dare.

"Go on," Sanjay said when she looked at him.

Joyce snatched the blindfold from Tom's hand and walked to home base. Then she put it on.

"Can you hear the other base?" Tom asked, and Joyce nodded. "Then walk toward it. I'll be right along with you."

"You don't expect me to run, do you?" There was fear in her voice.

"No, just make your way toward the sound. The ground is level, and I won't let anything get in your way." She walked slowly. Tom guided her twice, and she eventually reached the base. As soon as she touched it, she pulled at the blindfold and handed it back to him.

"I think you made your point," she said softly.

"Did I?" Tom challenged.

"Yes," she answered this time much more softly. "I could hardly walk a straight line." She stepped back from the base, and Tom did the same so they wouldn't become an obstacle.

"Yes. And Davey has to relearn how to do nearly everything in his life, including eat, drink, and walk. As frustrating as it is for you, because you want him to do well, it's even harder for him." Tom wasn't sure he was getting through with his words, but he was pretty sure his little demonstration had given her something to think about.

"Tom," Greg called, and Tom turned away from Joyce and jogged over to home plate. He handed Hanna back her blindfold, and they got the kids ready to take turns hitting. He did note that there was a lot more shouting and encouragement, especially when Davey came up to bat, and Tom shared a wink with Greg that was returned with a smile.

God, Tom loved it when Greg looked at him that way. Between him and Greg, they explained how the game worked and spent the next half hour giving each of the players a chance to hit. They did remarkably well. Davey and Heather were going to be power hitters. Kurt was much more tentative, and Tom worked with him closely, but by the end of the hitting practice, he'd managed to connect twice. Tom couldn't help grinning when Kurt jumped up and down after his second hit, and his father rushed up to him and lifted Kurt into the air with tears in his eyes. "You did it."

Tom blinked a few times himself, and he saw Greg doing the same. Sophia and Hanna did fairly well. For them, Tom was sure it was an issue of getting used to using a sense other than sight. He had little doubt that both of them would become good players eventually.

"This is amazing," Frank said once the batting practice was over. "They're really doing it."

"Yes, they are," Tom said.

"Let's try fielding," Greg said with energy. They gathered the players together. "Now we're going to place you each in an area of the field. We'll hit balls in your direction. The object isn't to catch them, but to pick them up off the ground before the runner reaches base. Now, you'll have to talk to each other so the others know where you're at. One of the important things is to learn each other's voices. In a game there will be people talking and other noise, so I want you to start by saying your name as you're in the field. Things like 'Sophia, and I have it,' or 'Davey, and I'm on it.' Also periodically just say your name so the other players get their bearings. Can you do that?"

"Yes," they all said excitedly, and the adults helped place the kids in position. Parents were nearby to help head off any potential collisions, and Greg began hitting balls to each player. The kids laughed, called out their names, and hurried for the ball. A few times they fell, but came up with smiles as they continued following the beep. Some collisions were headed off, and by and large the kids had fun.

"You all did great. Did you have fun?" Greg asked, and a chorus of yeses went up from the tiny team. "I'm glad. I think next time we'll do the same drills and then try to combine hitting and running to the base. Does everyone like pizza?" Another chorus of excited yeses went up, and Greg explained where they were all going to meet. "Once we get to the restaurant, we'll set up a schedule," Greg told the parents. "I'll also get contact information so we can stay in touch."

"I have a few questions," Frank said, and Tom turned to him. "How much does this cost? The equipment can't be cheap."

"All the equipment has been donated, as are the uniforms, pizza, drinks, and anything else we need. We're working to get set up as an official team within the league so we can be nonprofit as well. There are people looking into what needs to be done."

"How did you manage that?" Frank asked.

"I have my ways," Tom said, and he shared a brief look with Greg. "Let's get the equipment put away, and then we can get these players some pizza," he cried loudly, and the adults fanned out onto the field, including Joyce and Sanjay. Tom saw Joyce talking with Greg and wondered briefly what they were speaking about, but returned to packing up the bases.

A FEW hours later, almost everyone had eaten their fill and had left the pizza place. Greg, Skip, and Tom sat at the table with Davey, who leaned tiredly against Greg.

"I should get him home," Greg said softly.

"I'll stay here if you two want to talk a few minutes," Skip offered.

Greg shifted, and Davey sat up. Then Greg and Tom moved to one of the empty tables in the back. "Joyce sure changed her tune after what you did with her," Greg said.

"I thought she would, but I don't want to talk about her."

"Oh," Greg said stiffening. "Is something wrong?"

"No. I've missed you today. Skip and I went to the falls, and I stood at this great lookout point and all I could think about was you. I kept wishing you and Davey were with me."

"It used to be one of his favorite spots. We'd go there for the day, take a picnic, and when we visited the lower falls the last time, I let him row across. He was in heaven." Greg smiled. "When he was losing his sight, we did all kinds of things together. I knew it was likely for the last time, but I didn't tell him that. It won't be the same now, but eventually we can take him back."

Tom looked around them and then leaned across the table. "I want to come home with you, but I can't leave Skip alone again. Does Davey have school tomorrow?"

"No. He has the day off, but I have work that's piling up. Howard and Gordy are going to pick him up in the morning for me. Howard wants to spend time with him to help him with mobility and other issues. He also has an embosser and is going to help with reading."

"Are things happening too fast for Davey? He's had a lot to take in." Tom couldn't help looking over to where Davey and Skip chattered back and forth.

"I asked his teachers that, and they said he's one of the brightest students they've had. They say he shows frustration from time to time, though mostly they say that's because Davey still hopes he'll be able to see again. Speaking of that, I got a call from Davey's doctor, and he wants to meet with me and Sanjay late tomorrow afternoon." Greg shifted in the seat. "I was wondering if you'd go with me."

"Of course, if you want me to."

Greg glanced at Davey and then leaned closer. "I'm so scared I can't think straight. I mean, if there is something that could work, how can I say no? And yet there are probably no guarantees. What if we try whatever Sanjay proposes and it doesn't work? That would devastate Davey… and me."

Tom understood. "I know. On the one hand, you want to give Davey every opportunity to be able to see, and on the other, what if it causes harm? Nothing is guaranteed." Greg nodded very slowly, and Tom took his hand. "I'll be there with you if you want, and you can make the decision once you hear all the facts." Tom wished he could be more encouraging.

"Thank you," Greg said and stood up. "I have to get him home."

"I'll see you tomorrow," Tom said, pulling Greg into a hug. "I…." The words were on the tip of his tongue, but he held them back. He wasn't sure why. "I'll miss you," he said and pulled Greg tighter before releasing him.

Greg got Davey, and they said good night and left, with Tom and Skip right behind.

"Why didn't you tell him how you feel?" Skip asked once they were in the car.

Tom didn't have an answer, at least not one he was willing to vocalize. How in the hell could he say that the few times in his life he'd told someone he loved them they'd left or died, or worse, he found out they didn't love him back—only his money. He'd tried to make the words come, but they'd stuck in his throat. Tom glanced at Skip, who looked back to him.

"Believe me, I know what it feels like to keep your feelings to yourself." Tom knew from the way Skip stared that he was referring to him, and he winced involuntarily. "What you feel for Greg is written all over your face, at least for me."

"Skip, I can't talk about this. He hasn't said anything, and I…."

Skip nodded and turned away. Tom started the car and drove home, neither of them saying a word until Tom pulled into the driveway. Then Skip said, "Look, I'm going to take the chance that you'll bite my head off. But you don't want to leave Greg wondering. He deserves to know how you feel, and you deserve to know how he feels."

Tom growled.

"Damn it. That man loves you, but he's just as scared as you are." Skip shook his head. "Where is the Tom I knew who would do anything and was afraid of nothing? You'll take on setting up a baseball league for blind children without a second thought, or help libraries and parks all the fucking day. But you won't do the one thing that will make you happy, the one thing I wished I'd said years ago, before I lost my chance."

CHAPTER
Nine

GREG WAS as nervous as a long-tailed cat in a room full of rocking chairs. Every car that passed by out front had him jumping. Davey had called to tell him that he and Howard were having a lot of fun together. If he knew Howard, the wily man had figured out how to turn learning into games and had probably enlisted Sophia's help. Finally, he heard a car pull into the drive, and he peered out the window at Tom's red Ferrari. Right, Tom had told him Skip was using the BMW. Granted, on any other day he would have been thrilled to ride in the ultrafast car, but today he was too nerved up to really care about anything other than what the doctors would tell him. He locked the house and walked out to the car.

"It's going to be okay," Tom said.

"But...."

Tom motioned toward the door, and Greg opened it and slid into the seat. "Greg. What's the very worst that could happen?"

He paused. "They tell me they can do something to help Davey, I agree to it, and in the end, it doesn't work and his hopes have been raised for nothing. The best is that he gets his sight back, but I honestly believe that to be a pipe dream, and I hate the thought of anyone giving Davey false hope." Greg paused, and Tom started the engine. Greg told him where the office was, and they were off.

"I can understand how you feel."

They pulled up to a light, and Greg turned toward Tom. "Davey is just beginning to accept that he can't see. He's come a long way in a short time. Hell, I'm just starting to see glimpses of the sparkling personality he had before all this began. I don't want to lose that." Tom nodded, and when the light changed, they glided through the intersection. "I've been telling myself that whatever they propose, if anything at all, had better be more than some shot in the dark."

"What if it is a shot in the dark?" Tom asked.

Greg winced at the thought. "I keep telling myself I won't take it, and then I wonder how I can pass up any chance that Davey might see again. It's ripping me apart."

"With many things, the not knowing is the hardest part. The answer might be an easy one. I suggest you try to stop worrying."

Greg took a deep breath and nodded, settling back in the seat. He shouldn't have enjoyed the ride as much as he did. The car rode like a dream, and everyone stopped to look as they went by. Tom pulled up to the office and parked in the shade. They got out, and Tom walked with him to the door, lightly pressing his hand to the small of his back, just enough to let Greg know he was there.

"Mr. Hampton," the receptionist said as they walked in. "Please follow me, they're waiting for you."

Greg nodded and turned to Tom, who took his hand, squeezing it slightly. "It's going to be fine. No one is going to make any decisions for you, and you don't have to rush. You can hear the doctors out and then think about whatever they have to say."

Greg followed the receptionist back to Jerry's office, where both Sanjay and Jerry waited for him. They both seemed surprised to see Tom. Greg made introductions, and then they sat down.

"Dr. Patel has put forward an interesting treatment," Jerry began. "I have heard rumors and rumblings about this type of gene therapy, but I wasn't aware that it had been perfected." Jerry looked at Sanjay. "And I'm afraid it hasn't... yet."

"Can you start at the beginning?" Tom said.

Jerry looked at Greg, and Greg nodded.

"Of course," Jerry said and came around his desk to sit on the edge of it. "David's problem is genetic, and his condition affects his optic nerve. Actually, David was quite lucky, because he kept his sight longer than most documented cases of this condition. Most children lose their sight by five or six. His optic nerves have been deteriorating for a while, and it seems that in the last year it progressed more rapidly, leading to now almost total blindness."

"Okay," Greg said, taking charge. "What is this treatment?"

"Gene therapy," Sanjay said. "Since the mapping of the human genome, we believe we have a good understanding of which exact gene causes this condition. Basically, we would take genetic samples from Davey and try to repair the genetic abnormality using stem cells, then we would insert the corrected genetic material into his body."

Greg looked at Tom and then back at Jerry and Sanjay. "It sounds simple, but I know there has to be more to it than that. Will it actually work?"

"There's the rub," Jerry said. "In theory, since Davey's genetic material would be used, his body shouldn't reject it, but it's the body using the new genes for replication that's the problem. Basically, the body is meant to fight off anything that doesn't fit."

"And quite often it doesn't take unless…," Sanjay said, and Greg stiffened, knowing the "but" was coming. "I have had success helping patients." Sanjay paused again.

"I need to know all information in order to make a decision," Greg said.

"Many times, we have to go through the same process as a bone marrow transplant. In that procedure, we kill off the patient's bone marrow and then insert the corrected genetic material in order to guarantee that the body will use the new genetic code in the future. In this case, Davey's genetic abnormality would be corrected, and the body is often able to repair itself."

Greg stared, wide-eyed and openmouthed. Did he just hear correctly?

"Are you nuts?" Tom asked, half yelling.

Greg turned toward him and then looked at Jerry. This sounded like something out of a horror movie.

"I'm sorry," Tom said to him. "It isn't my place."

Greg caught his breath. "Isn't that what they do for leukemia patients? They kill off the bone marrow and then transplant. You want to do that to Davey?"

"It's the only way to replace his genetic code with one that doesn't contain the diseased gene. Then what we do is seed the area affected with stem cells so they will repair his optic nerve, and that will allow Davey to see again." Sanjay sounded so matter-of-fact, like you do this and this and this, and suddenly you have a cake for the bake sale. He made it sound so easy.

"What are the risks?" Greg asked, turning to Jerry.

"Quite extensive I'm afraid. It would involve killing off his healthy bone marrow and replacing it with what's been engineered in the lab. Granted, it's mostly his own DNA...." Jerry swallowed. "Look, I think this has possibilities in the future, but right now it's highly experimental, and quite frankly my ethics are screaming at me, 'Do no harm.'"

Greg nodded. "Would it be painful?" he asked, and he heard Tom inhale sharply.

"There would be some pain involved," Sanjay answered.

Greg stared at the two doctors, and without being able to think of any other questions right now, he stood up and shook both their hands. "I appreciate both your time," he said and then left the office with Tom behind him. With each step he moved faster and faster until he made it outside and gulped fresh air.

"I can't believe you're considering that," Tom said.

"How can I not?" Greg asked. "I know how it sounded, and I'm just as shocked as you are." He took another deep breath. "But if I don't consider it, then how can I sit down with Davey and explain to him that I might have given up his one chance to see again? I can't do that to him."

"Do that to him? They're talking about chemotherapy and radiation on an otherwise healthy ten-year-old."

"I know!" Greg snapped. "I was there. I heard every single word." Greg felt the last of his control start to give. "Damn it," he swore. "I was hoping this would be something real. But I still can't dismiss it out of hand."

"Come on, let's go back to your house," Tom said.

Greg nodded and walked to the car. He got in and closed the door. "What am I going to do? How can I tell Davey that I gave up the one chance he might have to see again?"

"Because that chance could cost him his life," Tom said. "Look, your doctor said there were ethical issues he wasn't comfortable with, and I can't blame him. Other than being blind, Dave is a normal, healthy ten-year-old. This treatment would cause him pain, and God knows what else, on the off chance he might see again. This is your decision, not mine. I'm just telling you how I see it." Tom started the car and pulled out of the parking lot.

Tom's tone told Greg all he needed to know. He knew what Tom's decision would be, and Greg wanted to make the same one. But he couldn't do that offhandedly, not if it could allow Davey to be able to see again. They rode in silence, Greg staring out the window and Tom driving, tension building between them. When they pulled into the drive at Greg's house, Tom barely turned to look at him.

"I just can't dismiss anything," Greg said softly.

Tom blinked. "I.... This.... This is so egregious and so outrageous. I just can't believe you're even considering it."

Greg shook his head. "Is it a sin to not want Davey to be blind? I know this is far out, and God knows I want to tell them no. But that would condemn Davey to a life of sightlessness. I also know it would raise his hopes only to raise the specter of having them dashed." He wasn't going to get through to Tom, he knew that. At least not right now. Greg reached for the door handle to get out and felt Tom put his hand on his arm. "You said no one was going to push me into a decision, but did that include you as well?" His tone was harsher than he intended, and Tom pulled his hand away.

"You're right," he replied, his tone equally biting. "You need time to make the right decision."

Greg got out of the car and closed the door. "Tom, I appreciate you going with me." He wished Tom would come inside with him, but he sat in the driver's seat without moving. "I knew this would be hard."

Tom finally turned. "Can you really be considering putting Davey through that?"

"I think I'm trying to figure out how I can say no and still sleep at night," Greg admitted before turning to walk toward the front door. He'd reached the front steps before he heard running behind him. Greg whirled around, and Tom pulled him into a crushing hug.

"Some boyfriend I turned out to be," Tom said. Greg hesitated and then reciprocated, placing his arms around Tom's back. "Sometimes I can be a complete ass."

"I'll remember that," Greg quipped. "Do you want to come inside?"

"No. Let's go pick up Skip at the house and then we can go over to Howard and Gordy's. I think you need to see Davey."

"Is this part of some plan to get me to make the decision you think I should make?" Greg asked.

"Probably. But I think you just need to see your son."

Greg nodded and let Tom guide him back to the car. "When does Skip go back to New York?" Greg asked as they drove.

"Tomorrow. I think he likes it here, but is too stubborn to admit it. So maybe he'll come visit again."

Greg felt guilty. "You should be spending time with your friend and I'm taking you away."

Tom grinned. "When I left he was Skyping with some friends in New York, and he can talk for hours. We're going out for dinner tonight. Skip talks like the world's biggest party kid, but he's a very private person, as well, and really seems to enjoy his alone time. At least that's what he keeps telling me." Tom began to chuckle. "I've always thought the clubbing and men were a cover for something, and after a certain conversation I know now I was right."

"What kind of conversation?" Greg asked suspiciously.

"He said he used to have feelings for me, but never said anything."

Greg rolled his eyes as they stopped at a light. "You're really oblivious. He still has feelings for you. I can see that. He tries to hide them, but in unguarded moments they come through."

"Damn," Tom swore lightly. "I'd hoped we talked it through on our trip yesterday." The light changed, and Tom pulled through the intersection. "How come you aren't upset about it?"

"If something were going to happen between the two of you, it would have happened long ago. He's your friend, and nothing ruins a friendship faster than sex. You're both smart guys and know that. It was also obvious that you're very close… but don't be surprised if he distances himself from you after he leaves."

"Yeah," Tom sighed. They pulled up to Tom's house. The BMW was in the drive, and Skip came out as they were getting out of the car. "We're going over to Howard and Gordy's and thought you might want to come along."

"Cool," Skip said and hurried back inside. Greg followed while Tom put the sports car away. By the time Tom joined them, Skip was ready to go. Tom locked the house and drove them all to Howard's.

Davey came out of the house and stood on the front stoop as they pulled up. "I knew it was your car," he called. "Is Skippy with you?"

"I'm here, you monster," Skip answered, to the sound of giggles. The two of them had somehow developed a thing.

"Uncle Howard is inside. Uncle Gordy is at the store," Davey explained, and dang if he didn't follow Skip inside, chattering the entire way.

"He certainly has found a friend," Howard said.

"I never would have guessed Skip would be interested in kids," Tom observed, watching them through the screen door.

"Sit down," Howard said. "Can I get you anything to drink?"

"No, thanks," Greg said.

"How did it go at the doctors? From your tone, I'm guessing not well." Howard shifted in his chair, and Token stood up, yawned, and resettled at his feet. "What did they say?"

"That there's hope, but the procedure is risky, possibly painful, and might not result in any change," Greg said, and then he explained what Sanjay had proposed. Tom reached over and took his hand. "I don't want to do it."

"Then don't," Howard said.

"But what if it's something that works and I'm taking away Davey's chance to see again?" Greg asked.

Howard was quiet for a long time. "It might surprise you to know that if given the chance to see, I'd turn it down. I'm happy with my life and who I am. Being blind is a part of me, just as much as being gay is part of me. Being blind will become part of who Davey is as well. And it's already happening. Right now Davey is outside with Skip, talking up a storm like any normal kid his age. He's also adapting amazingly fast. Sure, he wants to see again, but I will tell you that every risk should not be accepted in order to allow that. What they're proposing is invasive, potentially dangerous, and sounds borderline unethical. Being able to see is not worth Davey's life and potential happiness, because as you can see and hear from outside, he's perfectly capable of being happy as he is. And that's what ultimately counts, along with having people in his life who support and care for him above everything else. And I'm not just talking about you, Greg."

"Oh," they said in unison.

"You sighted people can't see what's in front of your faces. I can hear how you feel about each other in your voices."

Greg turned to Tom, and then they both began to laugh.

"I'm making an assumption here." Howard shrugged. "Sue me if you want, though you won't get anywhere against the blind guy, but saying the words only makes things better."

Greg didn't know what to say to that, so he kept quiet. Tom did the same, and soon they looked at each other and then at Howard before looking at each other again.

"For God's sake, get a room, I can feel the tension between you two." Howard stood up and took Token's harness. "Let's go out back. The fresh air will do us all good."

They stood as well and waited for Howard to make his way out of the room before linking hands. "I've made up my mind," Greg told Tom as they stepped outside.

"What did the doctor say?" Davey asked as soon as he heard their voices.

Greg had been wondering what he'd say to Davey and decided on a close version of the truth. "That there was a slight chance that you could see again." He sat down with Tom in the next chair and gently tugged Davey to him. "The things they would have to do would require more risk than I'm willing to take."

"But, Dad…," Davey began.

"No. I'll explain it all to you, I promise, but the procedure could be dangerous, and I won't let anything take you away from me. I listened to them, and you might hate me for it, but I don't think we should do it. Dr. Jerry wasn't a fan of the idea either." Greg hugged Davey to him. "I'm sorry if you're disappointed in me, but I can't risk losing you. I don't care if you're blind or anything else—you're my son and I'll be here for as long as you need me."

"Oh," Davey said softly.

"I know you're disappointed, but I'm not. I love you just the way you are, and you never have to change for me." His voice broke and he hugged Davey again.

"It's okay, Dad. I already talked to Uncle Howard about stuff." Davey patted his head, and Greg wasn't sure if he should laugh or cry. "Uncle Skip said he was going home tomorrow, so can we play beep ball again before he leaves?"

"We can play whatever you want, if Uncle Skip is willing," Greg said, looking at the others.

"Gordy will be home in an hour, and then we can all go to the park. It would do Token good to have some time to run, and you all can play." Howard settled in the chair. "Davey, do you understand what your dad tried to tell you?"

"Yes. I'm always going to be blind, like you," he said.

"Uh-huh, but that doesn't mean you can't do anything you want in life. It's sometimes more difficult, and we have to work harder, but we can do anything we want."

"I wanna be a professional baseball player," Davey said, and Greg knew instantly he was being a brat.

"Well, maybe anything but that. But you could grow up to be a professional beep ball player if you wanted, or a musician, or a computer programmer like me. Gordy is always watching those cooking shows, and he said that a blind person like us won. We have extra talents because we can't see. We hear better, smell and taste are sharper, and touch is more sensitive. All that will happen to you."

"I know."

"Well, what you don't know is that it won't take long before you forget what it's like to see. You won't need it anymore, and then when you grow up, you'll meet someone special like Uncle Gordy or Tom who will love you for who you are."

Davey laughed. "Uncle Howard, I like girls." He paused for a split second. "And I'm going to marry Sophia someday," he added in a whisper.

Howard chuckled, and Greg watched as he carefully pulled Davey into a hug. "I'd be happy to have you as a son-in-law, but you have to finish college first, okay?"

"Okay," Davey agreed.

"And you know that I'm here, and so is your dad, if you want to talk about anything. A lot of people think of being blind as a disability, but I never have. In some ways it's a gift, because we hear and truly feel the world rather than just see it. I knew I could do anything I set my mind to, and I took care of myself for a long time. You can do everything I or anyone else can—just remember that."

Greg wondered why he hadn't had Howard speak with Davey before. Heck, maybe they had talked together before and he hadn't been aware of it. He realized how insulated they'd become since Davey lost his sight. They'd been caught up in the minutiae of daily living to the point that he hadn't really explored any other resources beyond the beep baseball that Tom basically laid at his feet and the school where Davey went.

"I will," Davey said and then fell into Howard's arms.

Greg turned to Tom and smiled, relieved when he got a smile back and Tom moved closer. Everything was going to be all right.

"I said the worrying was worse than the reality."

"Yeah, it worked out. Now I have to tell Joyce and Sanjay and hope they leave quietly. She can be stubborn as hell when she wants something," Greg said.

"Give her a break. She just wants what she thinks is best for Davey," Tom whispered.

Greg figured the sooner the better, so he pulled out his phone and recalled Joyce's number before placing the call.

"What did you decide?" she asked, as abruptly as ever. "Sanjay said you didn't seem convinced."

"Then he was right. I'm not going to allow our son to undergo that kind of procedure. Davey is beginning to accept who he is, and I think that's better for him. In the end, it's too experimental and risky. I hope you understand, but I do appreciate you making the effort."

"He's my son," she said softly. "I know I've been a shit mother, but I wanted to try to help him."

"When do you have to go back?" Greg asked.

"Our flight is tomorrow morning. Sanjay has patients he needs to see, and I have appointments I need to make."

"We're going to the park to play ball in a few hours," Greg said. He would probably regret making the offer, but in his heart he knew it was the right thing to do. "You're welcome to join us. Tom's friend Skip is leaving as well, so we're all going out to play before he heads home."

"Davey does love the game, doesn't he?"

"He always did. I know it's not the same as when he was playing Little League...."

"No. It's better," Joyce said. "He's surrounded by people who care about him. He's playing with friends and family." He heard her sniff a little. "Yes, I'd like to come to the park."

"Then I'll call you when we're getting ready to leave," Greg said, and he hung up.

"Is Mom coming to the park? She won't play, will she?" Davey asked.

"She might if you ask her," Greg told him. He settled Davey next to him on the chair, and a little while later Gordy came home. He put away the groceries in the kitchen, and then everyone piled into the cars to head out to the park. Greg called Joyce, and once they got there, they set up the bases and got ready to play. When Joyce arrived, Greg watched as Davey nervously stepped toward her and waited.

"What is it?" she asked, and Greg stepped away, letting them talk privately. He glanced over every few seconds and saw Joyce pull Davey into a hug. Sanjay sat on the bleachers with Howard while the rest of them got ready to play, including Joyce, to Davey's delight. It was nice to see Joyce and Davey spending some time together. Greg didn't really trust her yet, but she was making an effort as far as Davey was concerned, and that went a long way for him.

"Can I hit now?" Davey asked after running the bases. They'd set up at one of the Little League fields not in use at the time, so Tom had put out all three bases—home, first, and third—and Davey, Joyce, Sophia, and Skip had been running between the beeping bases to get their bearings.

"Sure," Greg answered. "Sophia, will you help him to home plate? And I'll pitch." He turned to Joyce and Skip. "Would you two field? That way we can make it more interesting. All you need to do is pick up the ball before Davey makes it to base," he reminded them.

Tom got behind the plate, and Greg paced off the twenty feet to get in position to pitch. Gordy stood off to the side to watch and spot, and Sophia joined the others in the center of the field. Greg couldn't help smiling at the three blindfolded players, and when he turned around to look at Tom, his smile brightened, especially when Tom smiled back. Howard had been right. He hadn't seen it, but he should have. Tom's feelings were written all over his face. He stood there for a few seconds.

"Dad, are you ready or just standing there making goo-goo eyes at Tom?" Davey got into position with a little coaching from Tom and raised the bat, all set for the ball.

"Ready… pitch," Greg said and released the ball. It sailed over the plate, beeping as it moved. Davey swung and connected, and the ball sailed toward the outfield. It was a beautiful hit. Davey dropped the bat and took off for first base. He touched it and ran full-bore for third.

"I got it," Joyce cried, and it was only then that Greg realized he'd been yelling at the top of his lungs for Davey to go. They all had. Gordy, Tom, all the players and spectators who could see had screamed their heads off. Davey jumped up and down at the base, his excitement too much to contain.

"That was some hit," a familiar voice said. Greg looked over and saw Peter Crawford, one of the Little League coaches, walking across the grass toward them. "I'd love to have a slugger like that on the Tigers. Are you sure he can't see?"

Davey walked over, following their voices, and when he got close, Greg took his hand to guide him the rest of the way.

"That's the beauty of this game—you don't need to see."

"Have you found another team to play?" Peter asked.

"No. There isn't another in the area, and we aren't really a team anyway. This is just for fun."

"Well, if you want to play a game, we'll play you. The boys need to learn to rely on more than just what they see. Even regular baseball is more than just keeping your eye on the ball."

"Are you serious? I can tell you, this has a very different feel," Greg said.

"I know. But I think it will make them better players, and if the yelling, screaming, and laughter I keep hearing from over here is any indication, it seems like a lot of fun."

"Your players are welcome to join us anytime. We could have some games if we had enough players, and I think it would be amazing." Greg gave Peter his contact information. "Let's talk about how you'd like to do this." They shook hands, and Greg returned to his spot. "Okay, everyone, back into position."

They played for the next hour, with everyone taking turns hitting, or trying to hit, running, and fielding. There were falls and bumps, but they had an amazing time. When they were done, everyone was covered in grass stains, and though there were a few scrapes and bruises, smiles graced every face, especially Greg's, as he helped Tom pack up the equipment.

"I wish you and Davey could come home with me, but this is Skip's last night, and… I miss you. We were together that one time, and it seems like everything is conspiring against us."

"I have a lot of work to do tomorrow, but we can come over in the evening if you like, or you can come to our house. Davey is more comfortable there, and there will be many fewer issues with him getting around."

"Okay." Tom leaned closer. "I'll see you then." Tom winked, and a small surge of excitement coursed through Greg. They finished loading up the equipment, then everyone said their good-byes. Davey ended up hugging everyone at least twice, including his mother, and Greg thought he was going to have to pry Davey away from Skip.

"I'll be back again, I promise," Skip told Davey, and only then did Davey release him.

Greg guided Davey to the car and they piled in. Tom dropped them off at the house, and Greg wished Tom could have stayed. He stood outside and waved, watching until Tom drove away before going inside and making sure Davey got ready for bed. Then he worked for a few hours on a design that wouldn't leave his head before going to bed himself.

Greg had slept alone for years, but the bed now seemed big, empty, and lonely. He knew that was a ridiculous notion—he'd only spent a single night with Tom—but they'd been together a lot, and only now was Greg really starting to understand just how much Tom had burrowed into his heart.

"Dad," he heard as he lay in bed, staring up at the ceiling. He got up and slipped on a robe before walking to Davey's room.

"What is it?"

"I can't sleep," Davey said.

"Okay, roll over," he whispered and sat on the edge of the bed. He slipped his hand under Davey's pajama top and slowly rubbed his back. "Is that better?"

"Uh-huh," Davey said. And then the room went quiet before Davey said, "Do you love Tom?"

He skirted the question. "Would that be okay with you if I did?"

"Uh-huh," Davey said, obviously becoming sleepier. "Would he move in here with us?"

"Let's talk about that when the time comes, okay?" Greg asked, but he got no answer. Davey was asleep. Greg paused and then pulled his hand away, adjusted Davey's pajamas and then pulled up the covers. He carefully stood and left the room as quietly as he could.

Greg got back in bed and once again stared at the ceiling. Unable to sleep, he looked at the clock and sighed just before his phone vibrated. He jumped and answered it without seeing who it was, instantly wondering what was wrong. "Hello," he said breathlessly.

"Did I wake you?" Tom asked. "I couldn't sleep and hoped you were still up."

"No, I'm awake. I have been for a while. I just got Davey to sleep and I was getting to know all the intricacies of my ceiling. How about you?"

"Same," Tom said. "I really wish...."

"I know. Me too," he whispered. "I really wanted to thank you for everything today."

"That's what you do when...." Tom stopped.

Greg stilled. "When what, Tom?" He heard a sigh and nothing more.

"I really don't want the first time I tell you this to be over the phone. I want it to be face to face where I can kiss and hold you for hours afterwards."

Greg warmed and pushed off the covers.

"What are you doing?" Tom asked in a deep, rich tone.

"Well... I'm...." Greg could feel himself blushing. "I was about to... you know."

"I'd rather you... you know... when I was there to watch you."

Greg groaned and placed his hand on the mattress.

"I wish I could be there tonight, but I'll see you tomorrow, and I promise to make it worth waiting for." Tom hung up.

Greg placed the phone back on the nightstand. He sighed and smiled before rolling onto his side. When he closed his eyes, he found sleep came easily.

THE HOUSE was too damned quiet. Greg had spent the morning and most of the afternoon trying to keep his mind on his work. He'd only been moderately successful. Thankfully the design he'd been focusing on was nearly done. He had others he needed to start, but that wasn't going to happen today. Shifting at his computer, he pushed away thoughts of Tom and what he looked like naked before the house he was designing ended up with an obscenely shaped chimney. He worked for another hour and managed to finish the design, save the file, and back it up. Then he left and went to pick up Davey from his classes.

When he arrived, Greg went inside. He was met by Davey and his teacher coming down the hall toward him.

"I learned to read," Davey pronounced, beaming.

"I think he's had some help," Davey's teacher said.

"Yes, I think he has too."

"Davey is doing remarkably well, and I think with some assistance, he should be able to attend school with the other kids. He will still need special class time as well as classes centered around Braille instruction, but we'll try to make Davey's school experience as normal as possible for him."

"That's great," Greg said. "I really appreciate it."

"Both of you need to know there will be challenges, but we'll meet them head-on. Right?"

"Right," Davey said, to Greg's delight.

"Have a good long weekend, and I'll see you next week," she said. Greg thanked her again and let Davey show him how he could navigate the building and go outside to the edge of the sidewalk. Greg then vocally guided Davey to the car.

"You're doing great," Greg said.

"I'm gonna be okay, Dad," Davey said before pulling open the door on the passenger side. Greg stood stock-still as tears ran down his cheeks. Sometimes Davey came across as much older than his years. "You don't have to worry about me."

Greg got in the car and pulled the door shut. "You're my son, my only son, and as your dad, I'll worry about you forever. No matter how old you get or when you become the world's most famous beep ball player, I'll still worry about you. It's what dads do."

"Okay," Davey said with a shrug. "Can we get ice cream on the way home?"

"Not today," Greg said. "Tom is coming over, and I need to get home so I can start making dinner. You have things you have to do for class, I'm sure."

"Nope. I got it all done and I'm learning to read really good. Can I call Uncle Howard and see if he has any books or stuff I can read?"

Greg chuckled. When Davey got into something, he did it all the way. "I doubt Uncle Howard has things for kids, but I think we can find some talking books and things for you if you like. I can also look into getting you some books through the library. They have access to a lot of material for the blind."

"Really?" Davey asked, like the kid he was.

"Sure. We can do that tomorrow," Greg said and pulled out into traffic. The drive home didn't take too long. Greg was surprised to see Tom's red sports car parked in the drive. When he stopped and got out, he looked around, but didn't see Tom anywhere. He figured Tom must have taken a walk or something, so he waited for Davey to make his way to the door and handed him the keys to unlock the house. He'd been trying more and more to have Davey do normal things around the house in order to get used to them.

Inside, the house was just as they left it, and Greg wondered again where Tom was, until he saw movement outside the sliding patio door. "What are you doing out there?" Greg asked.

"Just waiting for you. I got here about fifteen minutes ago and was just sitting." Tom lifted a huge bunch of red roses from the table and handed them to him. "I wanted to get you something special and I hope no one has given you flowers before, because I wanted to be the first."

Greg grinned and leaned for a kiss, which he got along with a crushing hug that left him breathless. "No, I've never gotten flowers," Greg whispered, knowing Davey was probably listening to every word. "Let me put these in water."

"Hey," Tom began, stopping him. "I missed you."

"I missed you too," Greg said with a warm smile he couldn't help. "I need to take care of these and get dinner ready or we won't eat until later." Tom appeared disappointed, and Greg leaned close. "The sooner we eat, the sooner Davey will be ready for bed, and then we can be alone for the evening."

Tom kissed him again and then released him. Greg got a vase and put the flowers in it, added water, and then set the huge bouquet on the table. The room quickly filled with the sweet scent of the flowers, and Davey walked over, inhaling deeply. Greg was inordinately happy with the gift, and that kept a smile on his face all through prep and well into dinner.

"When are we playing beep ball again?" Davey asked while they ate.

"In a few days. It's supposed to rain for a while, so we'll play again when it dries out. I've called the parents of the other players, and we've set up a regular schedule to play each Monday and Thursday. We also have two more kids who want to play, so with Hanna and Sophia, we have a full team. To keep with the rules, we need to find a sighted pitcher and catcher who are the kids' age, but I think Peter can help with that, so it looks like we're officially off and running. We only have enough for one team, but I think that will change in time. Once word gets out, we'll have more kids and even some adults who might want to play, so it's all good."

Tom ruffled Davey's hair. "Did you have a good day in school? What did you learn?"

"I learned that he needs reading material," Greg said. "We're going to the library to find out what we can get tomorrow." He could not believe how things had changed in just a few short months. Davey was thriving, their lives were settling into a routine, and he felt more settled than he could remember. All of that was because of Tom; he could see that now.

Greg stopped eating and took a few minutes to listen as Davey told Tom all about his day and everything he'd done. Tom listened to all of it between bites with a smile on his lips. And Greg felt he really was one of the luckiest people anywhere.

He had a wonderful son, and a boyfriend who cared for them both. Greg hated to admit to himself as he sat watching them that he'd actually thought Tom would run for the hills once he realized what it would require to be a part of their lives. What amazed him every day was that Tom didn't only care for him and Davey, but demonstrated how he cared. Tom could be just as quiet and reticent about his feelings as Greg, but he'd already been showing both of them how much he cared. He'd pulled together this beep baseball team, buying the equipment because he wanted Davey to be able to have something back that Greg had thought Davey had lost forever. And he'd stood by him when Joyce was causing him grief over the awful treatment option.

"What are you staring at?" Tom asked softly and followed his gaze to the wall. "I like the paint color too, but I don't think it's that interesting."

"Dad always stares at stuff when he's thinking," Davey said.

"What are you thinking about?" Tom asked.

"I'm done. Can I go read?" Davey asked. Tom looked at him, and Greg nodded. "Dad said he'd see what kinds of bumpy books he could get for me at the library tomorrow."

"Bumpy books," Tom said with amusement, and Davey got up and slowly walked through the house, lightly touching his markers so he'd know where he was. "I cannot believe how far he's come. He can find his way around the house, and he's learning to read."

"He was always super smart, but this just blows me away. I know there's still more to come. There will be setbacks and frustration—I believe that's inevitable—but I couldn't be more proud of him," Greg said.

"Be sure to tell him," Tom said.

"I will, and you have to tell Skip that Davey is ready for him to visit again anytime. Somehow I think he helped him," Greg said. "He was someone who treated Davey like a person rather than a blind person. When you talk to him again, tell him thank you for both of us."

"Skip is just a big kid," Tom said before finishing the last bite of his meal.

Greg began clearing the dishes, then carried them to the kitchen. He put things away, watching Tom as he watched him. "It's always nice having people visit…."

Tom stood and walked over to him. "But it's nice when they go home too," Tom said, completing Greg's thought, and then moved closer.

Greg had dishes in both hands, and he somehow managed to get them onto the counter as Tom kissed him nearly hard enough to bruise. Greg could hardly think, and once he let go of the plates and didn't hear a crash, he forgot about everything except Tom's lips on his and the way Tom held him tight. Greg's brain shut off and he hugged Tom back, returning the kiss with everything he had.

"Does it make me a slut that after only being together once, I want you all the time?"

"No. What it makes you is mine, and it makes me damned lucky." Tom kissed him again.

"Dad, I can't get this to work," Davey called.

Greg groaned softly and stepped away.

"Were you kissing?" Davey asked mischievously as he continued toward them.

"Let me check it," Greg said. He took the tablet from Davey and turned on the speech-recognition software Howard had installed. "It should work now. When we see Uncle Howard, we'll have him make it so it starts up right away."

"Thanks," Davey said. "You can now return to sucking face." He giggled, and Greg tried his best to keep from laughing and failed.

"You're going to like sucking face yourself eventually," Tom said around his own smile. Davey shrugged and picked up his tablet, already searching for what he wanted. "I thought you were going to read."

"They only gave me the one book, and I only had a few pages left," Davey answered, and within seconds he'd settled on the sofa, engrossed in his story, foot bouncing. Greg shook his head and went back to cleaning up.

"It's almost bedtime," Greg said, and Davey huffed. But he turned off his story and worked his way over to where Greg stood.

"Is Tom sleeping over?" he stage-whispered.

"Yes," Greg answered and waited for Davey's reaction, but there was none. Davey hugged him good night and then did the same with Tom before heading down to his room. "I'll be in to say good night in a few minutes."

Greg listened as Davey cleaned up. "I'll be right back," he told Tom.

He found Davey in bed, waiting for him. Greg sat on the edge of the bed. "I'm so proud of you," he said. "You've done amazing things."

"For a blind kid, right?" Davey asked.

"No, for any kid. I couldn't be more proud of you if you had X-ray vision." Greg scooped Davey into his arms. "I love you more than I can say, and I'm so proud of you I could bust." He rocked Davey back and forth, tickling him lightly. Giggles filled the room, and then Greg settled Davey back on the bed. He was about to get up when Davey shifted and sat up.

"If you marry Tom, will you love me less?"

"Sometimes you ask the craziest questions. I could never love you less, no matter what I do or you do. It's the funny thing about hearts. The more people you love, the bigger they get." Greg hugged Davey and settled him in bed before leaving the room and closing the door most of the way. Then he quietly walked back to the living room.

The lights had been turned down, soft music played, and Tom waited for him on the sofa. Tom stood and met Greg, taking him in his arms.

"I'm not a very good dancer," Greg whispered once he understood what Tom had in mind.

"Neither am I," Tom whispered and pulled him close.

Greg went with it. The music continued, and they swayed back and forth together. Greg rested his head on Tom's shoulder and closed his eyes, letting Tom's scent and heat work their way into his soul. He loved every second of it, and within minutes he just held on tight and went with whatever Tom had in mind.

"We've been on the cusp of saying things to each other; I've felt it more than once," Tom said.

"Is that why you did all this?"

"No, I did this because I wanted you to know how I feel and that I don't take what I'm about to say lightly. Ken told me once how Patrick told him how he felt."

"I've heard that story too," Greg said.

"It's pretty amazing, and I knew I couldn't compete with that, so I decided on something more traditional. I wanted to tell you that I loved you when we were alone, like this, so you'd know I was serious. I love you, Greg, and I love Davey too. You're both the most amazing parts of my life. I knew you were someone special that first day at Ken and Patrick's party, when we talked the whole time, ignoring everyone else.

But I really know when I look at you. Just one glimpse and I want to smile." Tom lightly brushed his cheek. "I don't know what the future will hold, but I know I want you in it."

"Even with everything that comes with it?"

"If you're referring to Davey, then most definitely. Davey is a big part of who you are. You're a father, and I wouldn't have it any other way. He is one of the most amazing people on this planet, right behind his father and Howard."

Greg stopped moving. "Are you sure you're ready for everything being with me and Davey entails?"

Tom stopped moving as well. "What are you saying?"

"Nothing. It's just that being with me means Davey will come first. You're used to coming first," Greg said.

"So you're saying I'm spoiled?" Tom said.

"Well... yeah, Mr. Quarter-million-dollar Sports Car. I'm not saying I don't love you too, because I do. You wormed your way into my heart fast, but I'm worried I won't be able to give you what you'll want. I mean, there's nothing I can give you that you don't have."

"Except you," Tom said. "And, yeah, I think I can learn not to be the center of attention all the time as long as I get to be the center of your attention when we're alone. I grew up with selfish parents, and I vowed I wasn't going to be that way. Davey should be the center of your life, whether he's blind or not. I think I can live with being a little off-center...." Tom paused. "Wait, that didn't come out right."

Greg couldn't help laughing. "I think it came out perfectly. You are a little off-center." Greg smiled, and Tom scowled slightly. "Sorry. You were trying to be romantic, and I'm picking on you."

"You did say you loved me, right?" Tom asked.

"Oh yeah," Greg said, his chuckles dying as their gazes met. The heat immediately sent everything else from his mind. Tom leaned close, tilted his head slightly, and then kissed him. The touch was gentle and caring. Greg hummed softly as Tom slowly deepened the kiss. "I love you, Tom," Greg whispered when he pulled away. Tom kissed him again, more deeply, their passion building. Greg wondered if they were going to head down to the bedroom, but Tom simply held him, kissing and stroking his hair. "Are we...."

Tom began to move with the music once again. When the song ended and the room became quiet, Tom took him by the hand and quietly led him down the hall to the bedroom. Tom closed the door behind them. It was like they were in their own little world. Davey was asleep, and it was just the two of them—no worries or cares, at least for the next few hours. The ever-present tension Greg seemed to live with melted away as Tom pulled off first his shirt, then Greg's. They tumbled onto the bed together, kisses, moans, and soft whimpers filling the room.

"It's been a long time, but I want you. I want to feel you deep," Greg whispered.

"All in good time," Tom whispered in return, and then he proceeded to make good on his promise.

GREG'S SKIN tingled wherever Tom touched. Hours of soft, slow loving had left him wrung out, breathless, and covered in sweat, and they weren't done yet. Greg could hardly breathe and he didn't give a damn. All he cared about was Tom's touch on his skin and the way he looked at him. When Tom entered him after preparing him deeply and thoroughly, Greg thought he would split from sheer pent-up desire. His hands shook, and Tom finally began to stroke him, offering some hint of relief to the tightness that began in his feet and went all the way through him. "We waited way too long," Greg said.

"No, we didn't," Tom countered, snapping his hips. "We did this at just the right time. I love you, and you love me." Tom did it again. "Now I'm going to make you fly." And Tom proceeded to do just that, sending Greg on a trip that he swore took him to the moon and back. But the best part was afterward, when they showered together and then dried off and got back into bed. Tom spooned to his back, holding him tight. "Now this is perfect: happy, loved, warm, and content."

"It's been a long time since I've felt all of those at the same time." It had been, but Greg had the feeling the next time was just around the corner.

ANDREW GREY grew up in western Michigan with a father who loved to tell stories and a mother who loved to read them. Since then he has lived all over the country and traveled throughout the world. He has a master's degree from the University of Wisconsin-Milwaukee and now works full time on his writing. Andrew's hobbies include collecting antiques, gardening, and leaving his dirty dishes anywhere but in the sink (particularly when writing). He considers himself blessed with an accepting family, fantastic friends, and the world's most supportive and loving partner. Andrew currently lives in beautiful historic Carlisle, Pennsylvania.

Visit Andrew's website at http://www.andrewgreybooks.com and blog at http://andrewgreybooks.livejournal.com/.

E-mail him at andrewgrey@comcast.net.

The Art Series from ANDREW GREY

The Bottled Up Series from ANDREW GREY

http://www.dreamspinnerpress.com

Love Means… Series from ANDREW GREY

http://www.dreamspinnerpress.com

Love Means… Series from ANDREW GREY

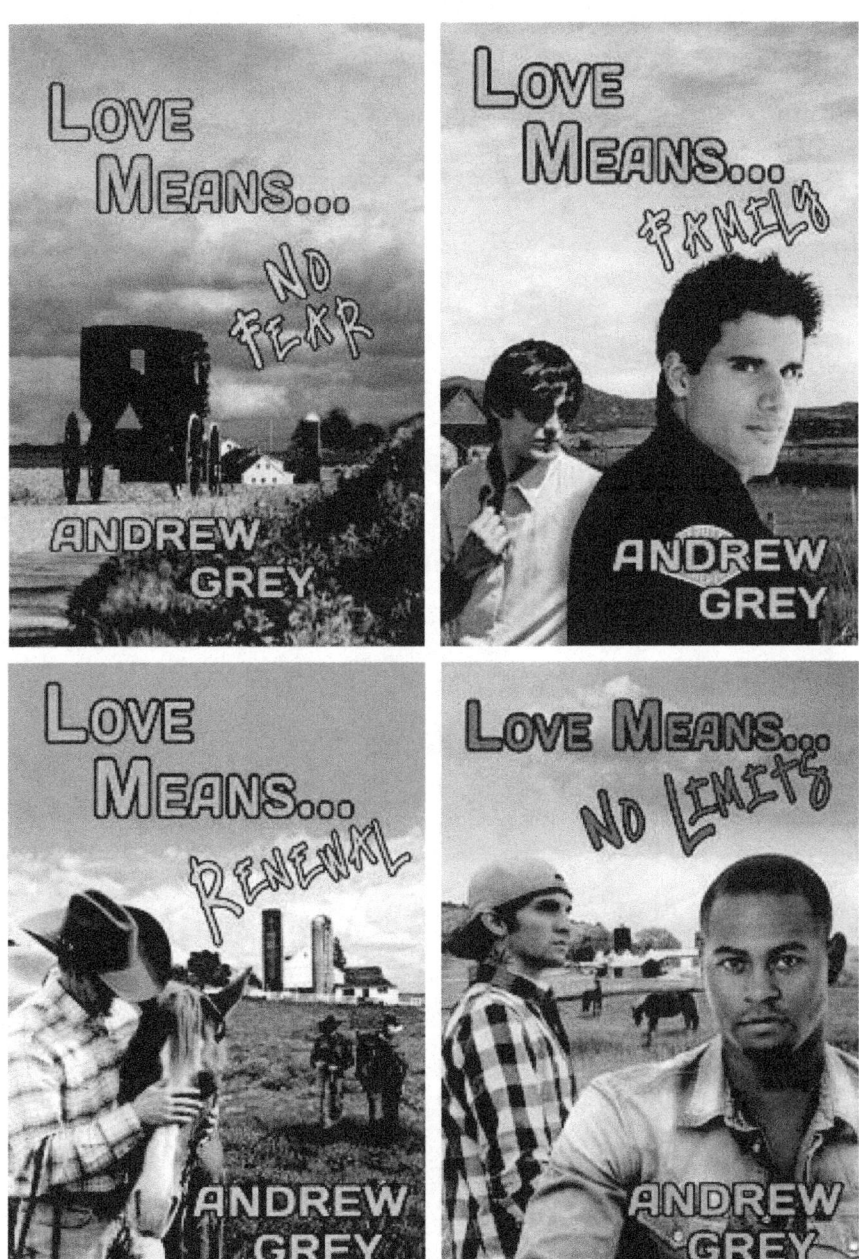

http://www.dreamspinnerpress.com

Taste of Love Stories from ANDREW GREY

Children of Bacchus Stories from ANDREW GREY

http://www.dreamspinnerpress.com

Good Fight Stories from ANDREW GREY

http://www.dreamspinnerpress.com

Stories from the Range from ANDREW GREY

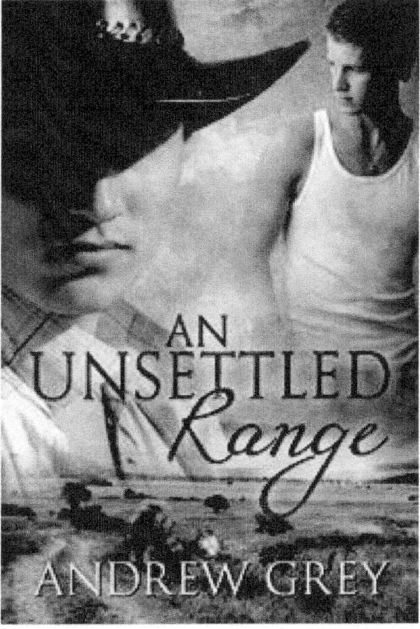

http://www.dreamspinnerpress.com

Stories from the Range from ANDREW GREY

http://www.dreamspinnerpress.com

The Bullriders from ANDREW GREY

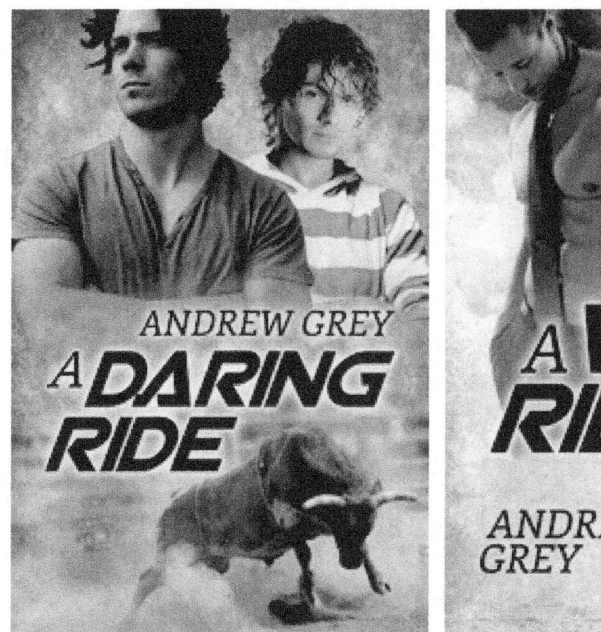

http://www.dreamspinnerpress.com

Senses Stories from ANDREW GREY

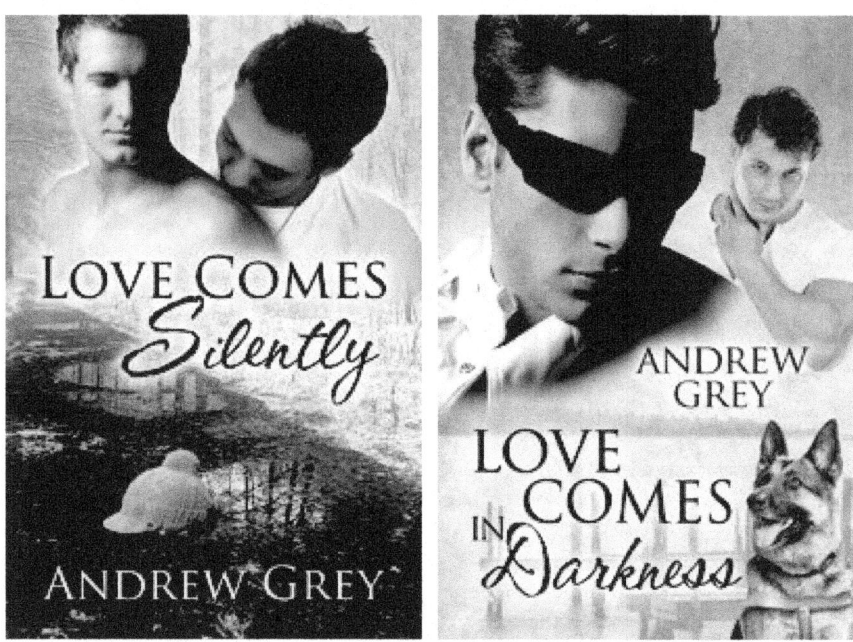

http://www.dreamspinnerpress.com

Seven Days Stories from ANDREW GREY

http://www.dreamspinnerpress.com

The Fire Series from ANDREW GREY

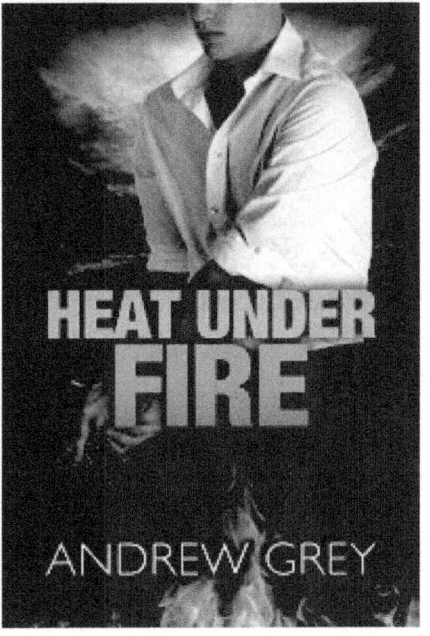

http://www.dreamspinnerpress.com

Work Out Series from ANDREW GREY

http://www.dreamspinnerpress.com

Work Out Series from ANDREW GREY

http://www.dreamspinnerpress.com

Children of Bacchus Stories from ANDREW GREY

http://www.dreamspinnerpress.com

Also from ANDREW GREY

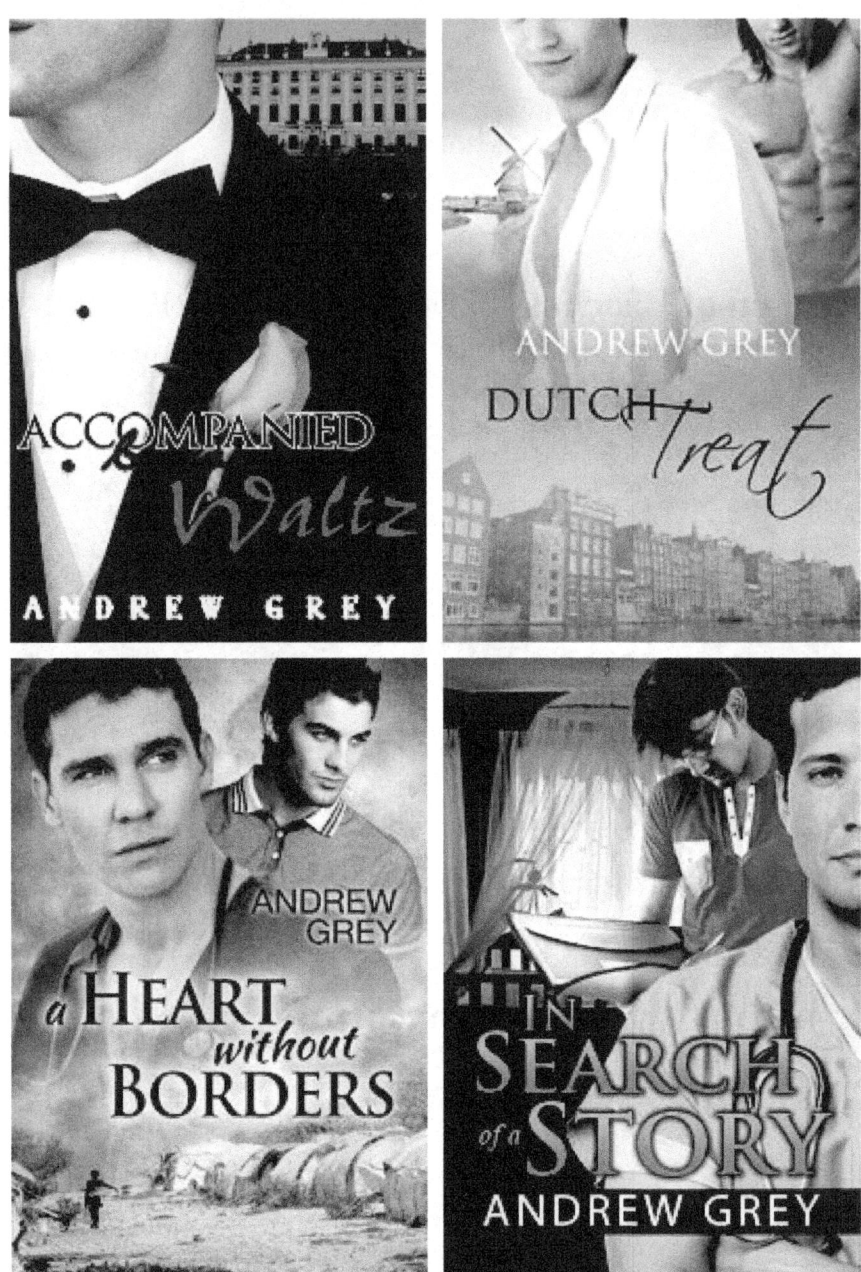

http://www.dreamspinnerpress.com

Also from ANDREW GREY

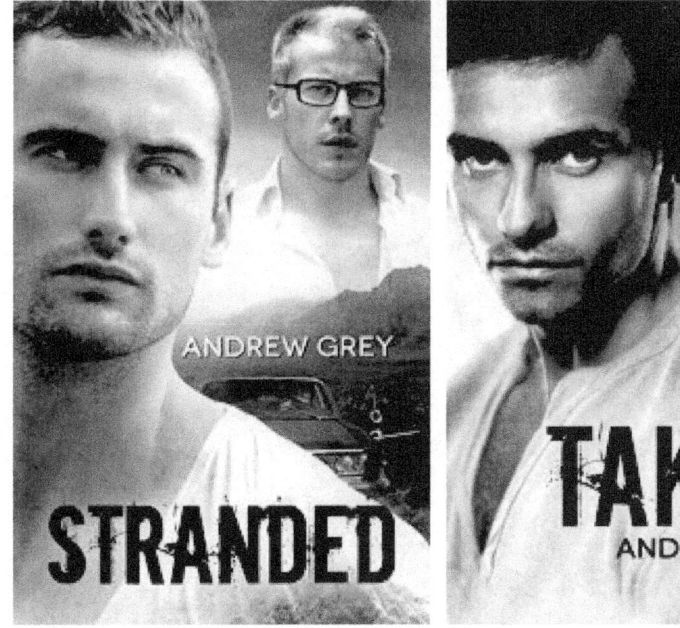

http://www.dreamspinnerpress.com

Novellas from ANDREW GREY

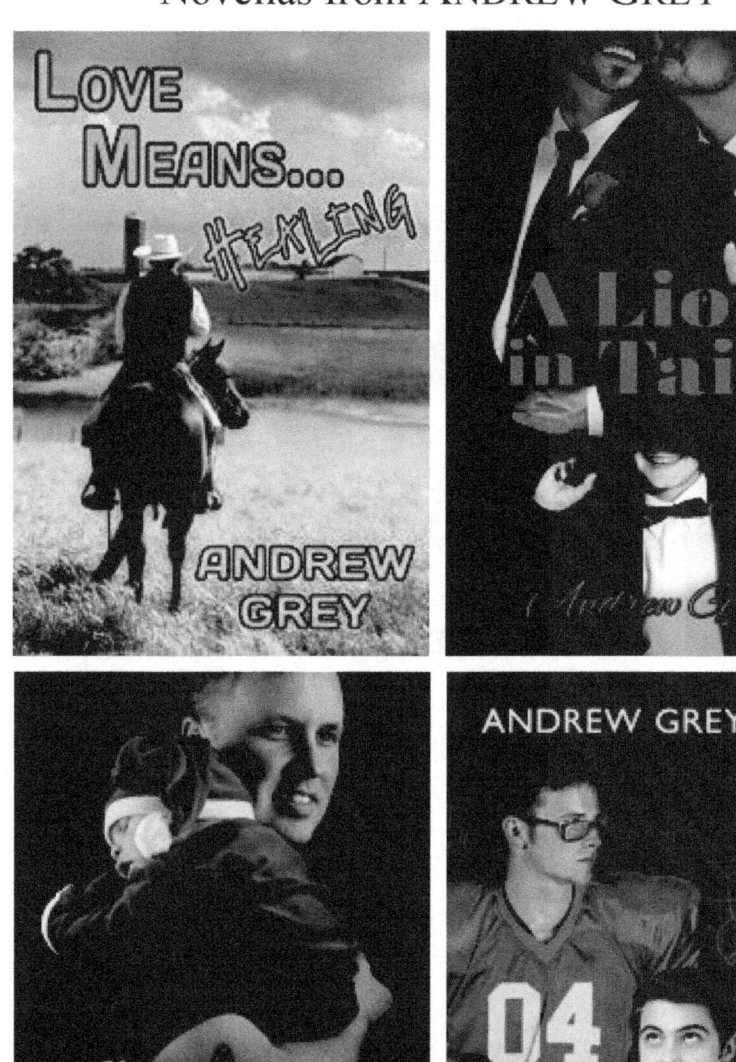

http://www.dreamspinnerpress.com

Novellas from ANDREW GREY

Dawn Kimberly Johnson

BUTTON DOWN

http://www.dreamspinnerpress.com

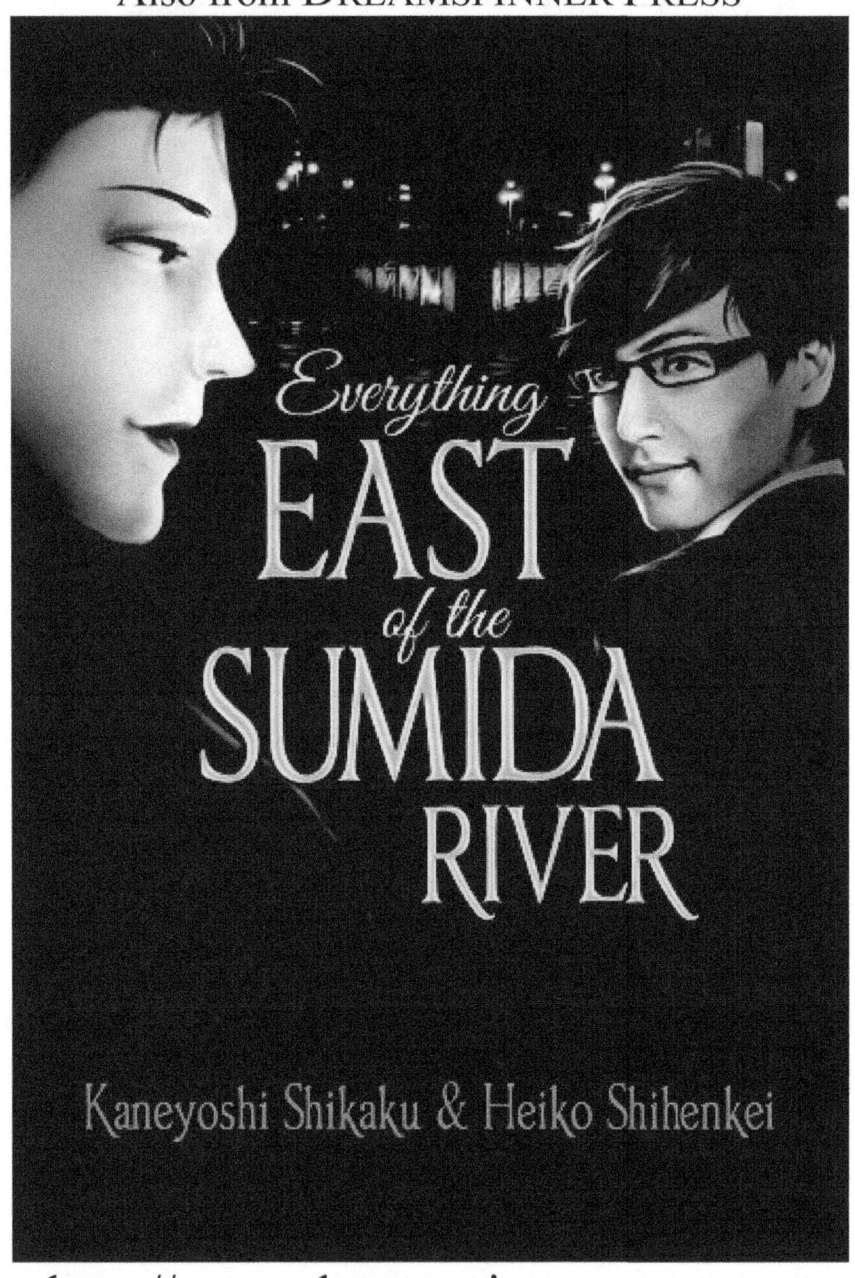

ASHLYN KANE

A GOOD Vintage